Fifty Shades of

Gorgosaur

LOLA FAUST

Contents

DEDICATION

To Neil DeGrasse Tyson

My endless thanks for your constant support. The admiration is mutual, my friend.

And to Kyle

who knows what he did.

TRIGGER WARNINGS, IN NO PARTICULAR ORDER:

Job interviews, "quiet luxury", billionaires, organized religion, disorganized religion, religious shame, youth pastors, Satan, hell, death (actual), torture (implied), taxes (implied), sex (including but not limited to oral, anal, manual, group, solo, dinosaur), light bondage, light spanking, sushi, Slavoj Zizek, Elon Musk, Kyle (any), prehistory, power, portraiture, raccoons, human resources, leather furniture, goats, animal death (goat), blood, true love

1

The bright morning light was promising to Alessandra. Today's interview could change her life. She needed this job. No, she didn't *need* it - she *craved* it.

This is a once-in-a-lifetime opportunity, she thought to herself. *I can't squander it.* Being the personal assistant to one of the world's richest and most mysterious billionaires, Tristan Black… wearing pencil skirts to the office, catering to his every whim, being in close proximity to that kind of power… what young woman wouldn't do pretty much anything to get that kind of position?

Anything, she thought. *Like getting out of bed. That's a good first step.* She sat up, giving her hair a bouncy shake, and pulled back the covers, swinging her legs over the side of the bed. She stretched and yawned, her satin pyjamas pulling tight over her firm breasts and taut nipples.

I hope Tristan is nice.

Tristan Black was world-renowned as a driven and laser-focused entrepreneur. Everything he touched turned to money. A rags-to-riches story, Tristan was also a philanthropist, spending nearly a third of his wealth on charitable work. Some claimed that the organizations he supported were significant to his childhood past, the details of which he had always refused to discuss, but these were only rumors. In business he was dedicated and fastidious, fair but tough, and was so obsessed with his work that he had no time to spend outside of his private office walls... much to the chagrin of the dozens, perhaps hundreds, of starlets, models and heiresses he'd rejected over the years.

All of this to say that no one had actually seen Tristan Black. Ever.

Journalists speculated as to who he really was, each one claiming to have heard the truth from a reputable source. There was the Midwest Billionaire theory, the Saudi Prince theory, the Elon Musk's Alter Ego theory, even a theory that Tristan was actually a woman who used the façade of Tristan Black to break the glass ceiling. These think-pieces circulated with nearly every news cycle, reverberating around the one question that was always on everybody's lips: who was the *real* Tristan Black?

Alessandra, however, particularly and unashamedly enjoyed the articles in more explicit publications. Whoever

Tristan was, the world had an active fantasy life involving him. People of all genders loved to fantasize about who Tristan Black was spending his time with in what exotic locale… and what he was doing to them.

At one point, she'd gotten her hands on an issue of Playgirl - most newsstands didn't carry it, but she'd ordered it online, and eagerly opened the manila envelope when it arrived. A writer who was identified only as "Jo" relayed her Tristan Black fantasies in detail. Jo imagined herself interviewing him in his opulent offices, playing a game of cat and mouse, and then making her his prey: bending her over his work desk and penetrating every one of her holes with what she described as his "juicy, thick cock". He tied her up and used her as his fuck-toy, spanking her and fucking her until he was completely satiated, and so was she. She never described him, really, but what did it matter what he looked like? He was rich and powerful. He could do whatever he wanted to her!

Alessandra blushed as she realized that her panties were getting wet from her arousal. She crossed her legs and looked around her. The other people on the subway hadn't noticed they were all in their own worlds, on their way to an appointment or to work or to some other mundane errand. She found herself wondering how many of them had their own secret desires. Was the young woman sitting across from her really a student at university, making her way to classes, or was that student on her way to meet her hot professor and confess her desire for him to fuck her senseless? Was the older man at the end of the train dressed up in a nice suit for work, or was he on his way to a dominatrix's dungeon, where a hot woman in latex would spend the evening whipping his ass until he could barely sit down in his cubicle?

No. These were Bad Thoughts. She'd been raised to be good and pure, unsullied by such wanton ideas. She'd gotten straight A's. She'd never had a drop of alcohol, never smoked a cigarette or a joint or anything else. Even her skirt had always been past the knee, long enough to avoid being dress-coded

Alessandra was so good, so pure, that she had never been touched. She hadn't even been kissed. She was going to save herself for the man that she married. Her virginity, she knew from Pastor Joseph's sermons, was the greatest gift she could offer her future husband. She would save every part of herself for her wedding night, when she would finally feel the hands of some as-yet-unknown but devoted husband caress her breasts, her thighs, the heated mound between her quivering legs.

But there were times when she just couldn't stop the thoughts. On these sinful days, she would read articles in

Cosmopolitan: stories of young women who went to sex parties, or orgies, or just swingers. She would wonder what it would be like to be filled up completely, mouth and pussy and ass, to feel each throbbing cock thrust inside her over and over again until she exploded. She would sit in her sinful discomfort, soaking through her cotton panties, begging a higher power to get her to her destination in one piece. Everything in her wanted to fuck the first handsome stranger she saw...

No. It was time to go to her interview.

As if on cue, the robot voice of the subway announced her stop.

She shook her head to shake off the erotic frippery of her fantasies and lock desire away, and stood up and exited onto the platform and out of the station in a small stream of people.

And then she was face to face with Tristan Black's corporate headquarters, Black Incorporated.

It was a towering entity of stone, steel, and glass, a monolith of Mammon, summoning the knowledge workers from out of their whirling weekends and into duty. The power centre of the city, its beating commercial heart. Its gleaming modern rooftop retreat had been the site of countless society events attended by the girls who always show up together at fundraisers wearing different dresses and all end up on each other's Instagrams – and there was also a secretive and extra-exclusive private members' clubhouse, according to rumors and winks, though no one would confirm.

The famous building had such a pull over the city that it seemed impossible that Alessandra would ever be invited to step foot into it. She hadn't the pedigree or the background. She wasn't a society girl.

And yet, here she was.

And here she would stay, with any luck.

A series of official looking men and women buzzed past her, smartly dressed and intensely focused. Her reverie broken, for a moment she was terrified. She didn't look like she belonged. Her pencil skirt had been thrifted from a charity shop in her hometown and her blouse, bought years ago, was from the sale rack of a JC Penney outlet. Her blazer was too long in the arms and was a slightly different shade of black than her skirt, and had a subtle nubbled weave that gave it ten points for visual interest but minus one million points for professional coordination.

Stop, Alessandra told herself. *You belong here.* If she did nothing but think of the negative, that energy would carry over into the interview, and she couldn't have that. She *was* qualified. With confidence, she could convince the shining bosses in their Loro Piana quiet-luxury cashmere socks that she was the one they wanted. She was sure of it.

Give me the confidence of a T. Rex in a herd of apatosauruses. Or a mediocre white man. One of the two. Let's go T. Rex, positive vibes only.

With a quick adjustment to her skirt and a flip-and-redo of her ponytail, Alessandra was ready. She straightened herself up tall, as tall as her old 3-inch round-toe court pumps could make her, and brought her shoulders back and down. Like the Pilates instructor had told her when she'd splurged on a fancy studio for a package of classes, which she'd loved but hadn't been able to afford to repeat. "Shoulders-back-and-down" had become her mantra since, in stressful situations.

With a final shake of her glossy ponytail, Alessandra stepped through the grand glass doors of Black Incorporated and into her destiny.

2

"Ms. Ironside," said a voice from across the room. "They'll see you now."

Alessandra sat in an airy and modern waiting room with a group of women. Maybe twenty, maybe more, each of them in something expensive and low-cut but somehow tasteful. Hair perfectly blown out with organic Kevin Murphy products at the salon. Makeup Sephora-perfect, cheekbones highlighted, lips with subtle work done at the medispa. High heels, mostly stilettos, a few with red soles. Pencil skirts that barely touched the middle of their sun-kissed thighs. Alessandra stared down at her court heels and sighed. She was outnumbered by a sea of beauties who looked like they'd been systematically built to get any job, any man. She tried the eye-contact-and-smile method of making friends with one of them, but her beautiful brown eyes just hardened, like chocolate unmelting.

Her internal monologue made a *womp-womp* noise. *Maybe coming here was a mistake*, she thought.

Which was why, instead of paying attention to her surroundings, she was deep in pretending to read the copy of *The Economist* that she'd found artfully tossed onto a low table. Bond yields were up, it seemed.

"Ms. Ironside," chided the voice sternly.

Alessandra looked up at last. The poised and beautiful older woman at the massive rough-hewn stone desk was looking directly at her with kind but firm eyes.

"Oh, my apologies," said Alessandra as she rose quickly from her seat and approached the desk. "Which way?"

The woman gestured to her left. Gosh, she was so gorgeous. Was everyone and everything in this entire place beautiful?

"Thank you so much. I appreciate your patience. I was so engrossed in an article about bond yields that I barely heard my name."

The woman blinked once, and seemed to regard Alessandra with new eyes, as if she was only just seeing her now as a person and not one of two dozen interchangeable beauties.

"Bond yields?"

"Yes, I was just reading about them in *The Economist*. Apparently they're up, and, um… there are differing opinions." *There must be differing opinions, right?*

The woman sat back in her chair and regarded Alessandra with the barest ghost of a grin. "I think you're interesting." She gestured down the hall to her left again.

Alessandra tried not to look back at what felt like thousands of siren eyes as she walked towards the hallway, which was across the airy, sun-filled space from the giant desk. Some of those girls had been waiting longer than she had. She wondered what it meant. One thing she knew for sure was that some of those stares had daggers in them for sure.

And then she was at the end of the hall, which ended in a massive flat rock face of polished pink granite, full of veins that curved gently into folds that looked almost organic, like the fleshy petals of the most beautiful flower, the one between the legs…

And standing in front of this luscious and lascivious natural rock-mural was a woman.

The woman was perhaps only a few years older than her, dressed to the nines in a smart gray suit that accentuated every curve in her luscious body. Her shiny dark brown hair tumbled down her shoulders and her eyes were an astonishingly bright green-gold. A pair of black-rimmed glasses perched on her nose somehow enhanced this woman's sensuality. She was young, she was beautiful, but she was nothing like the women in the waiting room; this woman was powerful and deeply mysterious.

She smiled tightly at Alessandra. "Right this way, please."

They walked down a long hallway surrounded by offices encased in brilliant glass windows. Each office window had a view of the city in all its glory - skyscrapers and condos flooded her vision with such awe-inspiring beauty that she temporarily forgot where she was going. The click of the woman's expensive heels in front of her, and the red soles on those heels, were a staunch reminder. Alessandra straightened her posture - *shoulders back and down* - and followed the woman into a private office at the end of the hall, on the corner, with two banks of modern windows and simple, minimalist decor that probably cost more than her parents' house.

"Is this Mr. Black's office?" asked Alessandra.

The woman laughed. "Oh, you won't be meeting him today. An eventual personal interview depends on how well you do."

A wave of confusion, nervousness and disappointment combined into one mega-feelingswave. Alessandra fought it off and tamped it down. Right now, she needed to focus. "I understand. He must be a very busy man"

"He is very busy, yes," she said. "And so I will be conducting your interview today. I'm Nellie Hammond, but you may call me Ms. Hammond."

"It's nice to meet you, Ms. Hammond," said Alessandra, extending her hand.. Ms. Hammond did not take it.

"As we just discussed, Mr. Black is incredibly busy," said Ms. Hammond. "Important clients to attend to and fly out to see. He is a genius of a businessman, but no matter how well a company is run, there are always fires to put out, and everything is urgent. I'm his executive assistant, basically his liaison for all of his business needs."

"But if you're the executive assistant, then why are you hiring...?" Alessandra trailed off, more confused than ever.

"We're looking for someone to do more of the... dirty work." An amused little grin played at the corner of Ms. Hammond's mouth. "Does that sound like something you could do, Ms. Ironside?"

Dirty work? "I'm not quite sure what you mean." said Alessandra slowly. This woman oozed sex. It *sounded* like she was talking about what the glimmer of heat between Alessandra's legs had begun to hope she was talking about. But this was a *job interview.* She needed to keep her cool. There were laws against sexual harassment in the workplace.

Ms. Hammond smiled. She opened up her laptop and looked at the screen.

"I have your resume here. It says you have a Master's in Fine Art. What made you change career paths?"

Alessandra blushed. "I need money," she blurted out without thinking, and immediately regretted it.

"Of course," laughed Ms. Hammond, sounding genuinely amused. "An MFA is hardly a lucrative degree. And what about this position in particular appealed to you?"

"It sounded exciting. To be the personal assistant of a billionaire. I'm sure there are a lot of things I could learn from Mr. Black."

Ms. Hammond's wry smile grew wider. "Oh. Oh, Alessandra, I'm *sure* there are."

Alluring and frightening at the same time.

What exactly was she meant to learn from Tristan Black? She couldn't know. She knew this would be an incredible professional opportunity. It would pay gobs of money. And she detected that there was something else she was supposed to learn from him, something that had to do with that stubborn point of desire that refused to be banished, even for a moment...

"You're nervous. Why are you so nervous?" Ms. Hammond gave her a half-smile.

Alessandra shifted uncomfortably in her seat, suddenly aware of how on the spot she was. And how wet. "I'm... I'm just nervous. I really want this job."

"How much do you want this job?

"I need this job, Ms. Hammond." It felt like the right thing to say, and it made Ms. Hammond's lush mouth quirk again, to which Alessandra's stubbornly swollen clit gave an answering throb. "I *need* this job."

"Why do you need this job?"

"Why does anyone need a job?" Alessandra asked, with her own slow smile. "For the money."

"This job specifically. Why do you need *this* job?"

"I... Maybe it's that if I work for someone like Mr. Black, it could open doors for me. I don't have a lot of money. I don't have anything really, but I want... more." Alessandra's voice strengthened as she spoke. "I want an interesting job. I want an interesting *life*. I don't want an ordinary life. I want adventure and fascination. And I need money for that."

There was a pause as Ms. Hammond considered and Alessandra held her breath.

"It's very demanding," said Ms. Hammond, finally. "You'll have to make yourself available at night and on weekends. You'll have to kiss your social life goodbye because at any given moment, you might receive the call. Whenever Mr. Black wants you, wherever he wants you to travel and how, you'll have to be ready. Do you understand?"

"Yes," said Alessandra. *I think I'm starting to understand.*

Ms. Hammond leaned over the desk, closer to Alessandra, so close she could almost touch her. For a brief moment, Alessandra caught a whiff of Ms. Hammond's perfume - an obviously expensive blend of rose and deep, woodsy musk.

"Do you have anything that would interfere with such a hectic schedule, Ms. Ironside? Any *one* who might interfere with your career?"

"No," said Alessandra. *And if I did, I don't think I would for long.*

The men in her life had been... disappointing, to say the least. A loser parade, if she was being honest. There'd been her high school crush, who had spent most of senior year chasing after her, only to ghost her after she refused to sleep with him on prom night. (Last she heard, he'd gotten some girl in the next town pregnant.) There was Kyle from college, whose couch she'd stayed on for a long while out of desperation when she moved to the city, who'd made it increasingly clear that he expected her to fuck him if she wanted shelter. She thought the big city would be better, the men more cultured. Instead it had been a giant pile of disappointment. The apps were full of married guys, thrice-divorced guys in their 20s, absolute weirdos, and an endless parade of boring men.

The one guy who'd actually been promising? He'd stolen half the underwear from her laundry pile while she was in the washroom, bolted out of her apartment, and then blocked her.

Ms. Hammond's voice snapped Alessandra back to the moment. "Really? You don't have a boyfriend?"

"No. I don't."

A wry smile. "No… girlfriend?"

Alessandra's face was now bright red. *How did she know I like girls too?* Alessandra had never told anyone about her desire for other women. How could she ever have explained to her friends - to her *parents* - that as much as she loved men's bodies, strong and musky and hard, she loved women's softness just as much?

"No. I don't have anyone. I never have," said Alessandra with a hitch in her throat. The woman across from her seemed to be glowing with sexual energy. It was all Alessandra could do not to reach down and hook a hand underneath her own skirt. She wouldn't, of course. But she wanted to.

Her clit beat in time with her heart.

"Surprising, given how you look," said Ms. Hammond huskily. "You're a very pretty young woman. You've got an incredibly intense natural charm." Her lips were swollen and glistened with some expensive gloss. Alessandra imagined Ms. Hammond's tongue emerging from between them, imagined Ms. Hammond pulling

Alessandra's chair close to her and tipping it back onto the ground, Alessandra tumbling out, and Ms. Hammond's curves pinning her tight to the stone floor, one manicured finger gently but firmly pulling her panties aside...

"Thank you," Alessandra breathed. Back to reality.

"So you're a virgin?" asked Ms. Hammond casually.

A bolt of unmet desire arced from Alessandra's nipples to her already-throbbing clit. She wondered if Ms. Hammond could smell her. She shifted in her seat, trying in vain to quiet the swollen need between her legs, marinating like a tender little steak in her own juices. "Yes," she said quietly.

Ms. Hammond nodded with satisfaction and leaned back in her chair. "Good. It's best not to have any... romantic entanglements when in this position."

"Why?" Alessandra asked before she could stop herself. Was she nervous or hopeful? Or both?

Ms. Hammond studied her for a moment. A ghost of a smile flickered at the corner of her lush mouth. "Well. Your schedule will be so packed you won't have time for anything else." Her fingernails tapped on the desk, glossy as seashells, and her green-gold eyes glittered behind her glasses. "There are other factors, too. But that's the primary one."

Those eyes. They seemed to bore into Alessandra's soul by way of her libido. The way Ms. Hammond looked at her, the way she moved languidly as Alessandra shifted under her gaze - it was intimidating, but delicious. Was this the way a mouse felt before being eaten by a snake? Marveling at the sun's glint on its majestic scales, before being devoured?

A snake. Of course. Like in the Bible.

She was Eve, and this woman was the apple. She was desperate for knowledge… desperate to know the curves of Ms. Hammond's body, the secret soft places, the scents and the shuddering…

…and then God would strike her down. Of course.

This was temptation.

A hot gout of lava-like shame burst forth from Alessandra's unresolved childhood issues and hyper-religious upbringing. It covered her arousal, burning it to ash, hot and charred and smoky. Her ears burned. Her face burned. Her nipples would not stop throbbing.

Even in her shame, she wanted. She desired… whatever this was.

"I will make myself available, Ms. Hammond. You can be sure of that. Available to Mr. Black, and to you."

There was a long silence. After what felt like an eternity, Ms. Hammond stood up from her seat and extended her hand towards Alessandra across the desk.

"Thank you for coming in today, Alessandra," she said. "I think Mr. Black will enjoy working with you. I know I certainly will. You start on Monday."

3

Alessandra floated like a woman in ecstasy all the way back down the glass-encased hallway to the waiting room, her heels clacking like gunshots on the stone. The waiting room was, perhaps, even more full than it had been when she'd gone in for her interview. Everywhere she looked, there were beautiful women, unattainable women, expensive women with their Peloton bodies and editorial-approved, sculpted faces.

For a moment she was overcome with an overwhelming self-doubt, as if she'd been cast in a starring role in a Broadway musical that every other wannabe starlet had long coveted. She'd won the game they were all here to play, and she'd come from behind. She was a long shot.

But sometimes long shots pay off.

She'd won. Did it really matter why?

"Everyone still seated, you are all dismissed," came Connie's voice from behind the stone desk.

Thousands of blank siren eyes swiveled toward Alessandra, each pair trying to process what had just happened. Alessandra imagined what they must be thinking? *That girl? She's not even that pretty. I'll bet she doesn't even do Pilates. What are those shoes? Her purse is from Aldo or something. Bet she slept with someone. What a whore.*

It was normally a train of thought that would end with Alessandra curled up in shame, beset on all sides by memories of her parents and her peers and her youth pastors screaming about how she was a whore, girls are whores, women are *Whores of Babylon*. And yet somehow, today, it was different. Those thoughts battered against the glass, but they didn't come in.

It was as if she was in a glass hallway in her mind, just like the one that had led her to the opportunity of a lifetime. And nothing outside of it could hurt her.

She beamed a smile at the waiting women, pretending innocence. "Sorry," she mouthed.

One by one, they slowly rose from their seats and made their way towards the exit, some of them throwing cold and catty glances in Alessandra's direction.

Alessandra was too giddy with excitement and goodwill to care. She hoped that they each found their own billionaire to serve, but this one was *hers*. She'd done it.

Is this what success feels like? If so, she wanted a lot more of it.

As she made her way out of the building onto the subway platform, and then onto the train, Alessandra couldn't stop herself from smiling. *I must look nuts,* she thought to herself, *or like a serial killer or something.*

But she was beyond caring about how she looked. This was one of the best days of her life. She beamed. She was finally making something of herself, digging herself from the trenches of her uninspiring hometown and making her mark in the big city. It could be everything she'd ever dreamed of, opening doors to a life of luxury and a world of endless possibilities…

Suddenly, she noticed a pair of eyes on her.

Sitting across from her was a handsome man in a tailored business suit, his eyes wandering over her face for the source of her happiness. He looked out of place, like a Rolex billboard towering over a rundown apartment block. He oozed wealth and refinement from every pore. What was he doing taking the subway? For kicks, to see what it was like to rub elbows with regular folks so he could remember what life was like before he made it to the top? Maybe he'd been born into privilege and was just slumming it to tell his buddies at the golf club. She glanced at his hand - no wedding ring. And at his wrist: was that a Patek?

Maybe this was the famous Mr. Black?

No. His briefcase monogram was wrong: ALW.

But what in the world was he doing here? Maybe he was a mirage? That must be it. Maybe she was dreaming all of this - the interview, the new job, everything.

Alessandra was about to look away when he smiled at her, a subtle half-smile that was undeniably sexy.

Alessandra's face grew hot.

He must have noticed that she was blushing, because his smile grew wider, a set of dimples suddenly appearing as if by magic. *How is it even possible for him to be hotter?* Before she could stop herself, she found herself thinking about what it would be like to follow him to his next stop. How she would ask him if he'd like to have coffee with her, since he seemed to find her so *fascinating*. And after coffee, she'd suggest that they "go back to his place" like they always said in movies.

Alessandra wondered what he tasted like, if each part of his body would taste different. She wondered what it would be like to lick the insides of his wrists, to take off that watch and kiss the tender part where his heartbeat shuddered beneath his skin. She wondered what his voice would sound like as she slowly sank to her knees before him. Her inner tigress, the part of her that wanted all of it, roared in time with the screech of the train wheels, the chatter of the passengers, her heart that raced faster and faster with every *chug* of the train and *thunk* of a passenger's knee hitting cold metal as they stumbled.

Her senior year of high school, shortly after she turned eighteen, she'd seen a porn clip on some shady website at a friend's house. They were hiding from their parents, of course, who thought that these very good, very demure girls were doing Bible study in the basement.

The two girls laughed at how strange the film was, how deeply bizarre the present scenario. A deliveryman rang the doorbell and the woman in the house was in lingerie… why? Just sitting around in lacy underwear and a bra? They didn't seem to know each other, and they had little in common. The woman was beautiful in a plastic, artificial way, as if her face had been created by AI, and the man was handsome in a blue-collar way, though he looked like he would smell faintly of the cheap beer her father drank when her mother wasn't home.

And yet… here he was fixing her television, and then the television turned on, blaring, with the sounds and sights of a different man and a different woman deep in the throes of some very graphic sex. The man pounded his hard dick into the woman's ass, over and over as she moaned in pain-pleasure. It was almost metaphysical, the postmodern image of the porn couple watching the porn couple, while the audience stared at the carnivalesque spectacle, their own gussets slowly soddening.

The repairman, of course, reached out and fondled the woman's breast, which led to a brief kiss, and the woman whispering "I'm a virgin" in her best attempt at docility, followed by a much less brief encounter on the couch, moaning in concert with their own porn-watching. As if to say, don't worry, friends, we all do it.

Pornography is normal. So is lingerie. So are orgasms.

Alessandra couldn't help it. She'd found it erotic, that picture-in-picture, sex-in-sex. She wanted someone to come to her door, fix her TV, and attack her clit with his tongue, her hot wet flesh with his hot hard cock.

Now, staring at this stranger on the train, she pictured herself in lingerie, legs spread wide for the thick cock of the man in front of her, taking each powerful thrust into her tight passion-tunnel until she screamed. How would it feel? Would it hurt? Would it be too much for her to handle, or would she thrive in the moment? Would she think of that porno, sex-in-sex-in-sex?

"I'm a virgin," she'd whisper, just like the girl in the porno. For her, unlike the plastic actress, it was true. But Alessandra knew that, given the opportunity, her inner tigress would claw her way out of the Bible-study basement in her soul and get herself speared like a hot dog at a beach barbeque.

The subway chimed for her stop. Alessandra gave the man a tight smile, then leapt from her seat, leaving the gorgeous stranger behind with the lustful thoughts of what could have been, her panties soaked through for the second time that day.

No romantic entanglements. I'll be busy.

Perhaps with Ms. Hammond.

Or the elusive Mr. Black.

She certainly wasn't in Bible study anymore.

Alessandra fell into bed, still giddy. It would be everything she'd always wanted, this job. This was her ticket to the happy life she'd always wanted: money, excitement, meaningful work. She'd lived for far too long as Cinderella:

a childhood of restriction and chores to "build character", a teenagehood of lectures and grounding and Bible study instead of extracurriculars and dates and parties. Then came early adulthood: working hard for people who didn't appreciate her, who wrote her up for arriving two minutes late and who microwaved leftover fish in the break room.

But now? Cinderella was invited to the ball. This job was the one thing that could alter her life forever. It was her big chance. It could transform her into the graceful, elegant woman who was the envy of the crowd. It already had.

I wonder if Tristan Black is my Prince Charming?

Maybe Ms. Hammond is my Princess Charming, too. Maybe they're both in on it.

She let her mind wander to the man on the train. There was something about him that immediately caught her attention - was it his smart, tailored suit? His eyes? The way he smiled when he noticed that she was looking at him? Or was it how he looked at her, the coy demeanor that quickly evolved into an insatiable hunger that devoured her in a singular glance?

Her upbringing told her that she must be pure, righteous. There was no place for dirty thoughts in the enclosure of her youth.

And yet, her inner tigress was hungry.

Why now? Was it the thought of working for Tristan Black, the mysterious billionaire playboy, who could make all of her earthly desires come true? Well… most of them?

And if he could give her the career, the money, the security… what else could he give her?

She suddenly understood "Jo" quite a lot better.

The blinds were closed. Night had descended upon the city. There was no one around to see, no parents to shame her, no jealous and angry God in His sky-castle to peek between the clouds and cast her into the fires of hell for her carnal sin. Slowly, carefully, Alessandra let her hand drift down below the waistband of her pyjama pants and inside her panties.

She closed her eyes. Waiting for her in the darkness was Tristan Black, reclining on a leather coach, shirt unbuttoned as he watched Alessandra dance in front of him.

"Dance for me, Alessandra," whispered her handsome fantasy. *"It's okay. I want you to."*

Alessandra danced slowly and sensually, eyes half-lidded. His gaze bore into her until she began undressing herself: her blouse, her skirt, her lacy lingerie that she let drop seductively to the floor. His eyes darkened with lust:

this fantasy man was hungry, wild for her. Every part of him was burning with an unmitigated need to have her.

Alessandra's inner tigress growled. This was her moment. This was what she'd always wanted, but had been too afraid to claim, too beaten down by the spectre of sin and hell. *No longer,* her tigress roared. *This is my time.*

Alessandra rubbed her clit in circles, tension and pleasure building and building. as she pictured herself sitting on her fantasy man's lap. The elusive Tristan Black. He looked like the man on the train, but also unlike him: a perfect hybrid of the man and her own personal vision of ultimate power and desire. He removed his belt and looped it around her body, pulling her closer. She moaned at the thought of him holding her with such authority. He pulled his rock-hard cock out of his pants and, looking into her eyes with his lustful gaze, thrust it inside her dripping wet pussy.

The fantasy was so powerful that she could almost feel every thrust moving hard and fast inside her, so deep that she could barely contain the mounting orgasm that threatened to escape at any moment. "*More...*" she whispered.

Her inner tigress had been let loose. The fantasy man, her insatiable Tristan Black, pulled Alessandra up before bending her over in front of him and pushing his cock into her tight little asshole. She was so wet, so incredibly wet, that it slid in without a bit of resistance. She cried out in shocked pleasure from the force of it. As he moved inside her little ass, Alessandra rode a wave of absolute bliss, sending an arc of electric ecstasy into her beleaguered clit.

And then, unbidden, Alessandra's fantasy changed.

As Tristan pounded her, there was suddenly a mirror in front of her. Her reflection was familiar, albeit possessed by unbelievable pleasure, but Tristan himself had changed. Instead of the handsome stranger, she now pictured a large... beast? Tristan had become a huge reptilian creature that gnashed its razor-sharp jaws in time with its thrusts, a creature that screeched in delight as he fucked Alessandra harder and harder.

Something about that vision pushed her over the edge.

Alessandra arched her back. The fantasy was bubbling over in her mind and pouring forth into her body as her orgasm tore through her like a sharp talon. A muffled, strangled scream escaped Alessandra's lips, alongside the most intense and powerful orgasm she ever experienced.

Satiated and confused, she slowly let her body go limp and her eyes gaze up to the ceiling. All that remained in that room was the sound of the fan above her and the traffic from outside her window, honking and squealing rubber echoing from the earth below. Somewhere, near the garbage bins, a raccoon was rummaging through the day's trash.

What the fuck was that, inner tigress?

But her inner tigress was asleep. It had been a very busy evening for her.

That was crazy, thought Alessandra. It was true that her fantasies were often wild; a strict upbringing could create an outsize and bizarre erotic response, she knew from the psychology course she'd taken in college. But a *reptilian creature*? That had never been part of her interior landscape.

Maybe it's lack of sleep?

That must be it, she thought as she reached out with a weary hand to turn out the light.

Questions about ass-fucking lizards could wait. She had an important interview tomorrow.

4

Alessandra had bought a new outfit for her first day of work.

It was a Dolce & Gabbana skirt suit; she'd seen it in the window of the designer consignment store a few blocks from her apartment. Even secondhand, it had been the largest single purchase she'd ever made. *But it was worth it*, she thought, admiring her reflection in the window of her new office. The skirt was a little shorter than she would have normally worn, fluted and flared at the bottom with masterful tailoring, and the gorgeously fitted suit jacket had a hem to match. A cream silk-satin button-down blouse skimmed over her skin with the gentlest of touches. She'd eschewed the showy gaudiness of Louboutin heels after reading a Lainey Gossip article on "quiet luxury" and thrifted a pair of vintage Ferragamo three-inch pumps instead, spending an hour with leather conditioner and shoe polish until they were mostly restored. Mostly, because she wanted to be appealing enough that Tristan Black would find her alluring, but not so much that she looked like she was trying too hard.

Was it trying too hard to try not to try too hard?

At the very least, I know I can *dress the part.*

She felt odd at first, it was true. Vanity was one of the cardinal sins, according to her parents and her pastor. Especially her pastor.

"Do you want to be beautiful?" boomed Pastor Joseph from the lectern when she was thirteen, looking straight at her. "Beauty is the first step towards *hell.* Do you want to be sexy? Sexiness is the first step towards *hell.* Be modest, or pay the price. Vanity is an ugly, ugly habit."

But on that day, as she stood on the edge of an enviable new life, vanity was something that she could afford.

And although she would never tell anyone, Alessandra *liked* how she looked. She found her successful self sexy. There was something more sensual about her that day, something that the other men and women in the office were noticing, too.

She smiled. Her office was on the 104th floor of the Black Incorporated tower. Beyond her reflection, the city stretched languidly, lazily all the way to the river and beyond. Tiny cars ferried tinier people hither and yon, like ants in an ant farm. Like plankton in the sea. Masses and masses of them, each one with their own mission.

Alessandra towered over them all now.

On top of the world.

And she had to be on the top of her game, too. For Tristan Black.

The brittle slam of a glass door interrupted Alessandra's reverie. She whirled, startled. There stood Ms. Hammond, a vision of corporate grace, her hair done up in a sleek bun so perfect it could have been sculpted by God Himself.

Ms. Hammond was still the sexiest woman she'd ever seen. Her perfect lips, her soft skin, her tumble of hair, her knowing smile, her arresting green-gold eyes… and her *body*. The lushness of her hips. Her breasts that threatened to spill over, like a cup filled to the brim and held in place only by surface tension. She was wearing a tight burgundy leather skirt suit with a snakeskin-print silk blouse and Saint Laurent stillettos.

Ms. Hammond gave her a signature smirk-smile and reached forward to shake Alessandra's hand. Alessandra fought an increasing urge to press her own perfectly made up lips to Ms. Hammond's. *No. I can't. I need this job. And if this is the assistant, what must Mr. Black be like…?*

"It's good to see you, Ms. Ironside," said Ms. Hammond in her low and husky voice. "I trust you slept well before your first day."

Alessandra thought back to the night before, and smiled. "Oh yes, very well," she answered.

"That's good to hear. It's going to be a busy day. We don't have a lot of time to stand around and chat."

Without another word, Ms. Hammond turned on her stiletto heel and exited the room. Alessandra caught on that she was meant to follow. She all but ran to keep up with Ms. Hammond's steady stride, past offices full of staring men, past boardrooms packed with people in suits: powerful people, Alessandra assumed, making tough business decisions about billion-dollar mergers.

Alessandra speedwalked alongside Ms. Hammond, trying not to fall over in her Ferragamos, until they reached a long hallway that felt different from the rest of the office. There was a quietude about it, an air of reverence. An enormous painting seemed to mark the juncture: it was taller than Alessandra and nearly seven feet wide. It seemed to be a deeply impressionist portrayal of a jungle, all greens and browns and sunlight-gold dapples, but interrupted with a

41

shower of red that slashed across the canvas like a wound. Like blood.

It probably cost more than my parents' house, she marveled.

At the end of the hallway stood a set of heavy wooden doors that looked antique, as if they'd been carried off from a castle in the Scottish highlands.

"We'll be in here for the day," said Ms. Hammond. "It's somewhat removed from the rest of the office, so we'll have plenty of quiet. You'll see why that's essential."

A day with Ms. Hammond in a quiet spot, uninterrupted, sounded like Alessandra's version of heaven. Much more so than angelic choirs and celibacy.

Or Ms. Hammond's boss.

"Is Mr. Black in this office?" asked Alessandra.

Ms. Hammond turned towards her, the wry smile intact. "You're so... *enthusiastic.* Why do you think Mr. Black would be behind these doors?" Her tone was amused, but not unkind.

There was a long pause. It was an odd question; wasn't Alessandra was there for the sole purpose of working for Tristan Black?

And yet, he was an incredibly busy multi-billionaire. Wouldn't it make sense that he wasn't in the office from time to time?

"I suppose I thought he might be around for my first day."

Ms. Hammond chuckled. She pressed her thumb to a barely perceptible red dot to the left side of the door; it swung open to reveal a futuristic-looking glass panel, onto which she entered a long and complicated passcode. The doors swung open, slowly and smoothly, to reveal an enormous private office.

The office was an altar to masculinity and wealth. An enormous mahogany desk dominated the wall across from the door, with a huge leather wingback chair behind it and four smaller chairs in front, facing it. Above the chair hung a giant wooden mask, intricately carved into the shape of a giant reptile's head, tongue out and teeth bared. Built-in wooden bookshelves lined the walls to the right and left, filled with vintage-looking books punctuated by sculptures made from soapstone or metal or wood or glass, and a giant caramel-leather sofa sprawled across most of the length of the room to her left. The place smelled like woodsmoke and cigars.

Unlike the rest of the office building, there were no windows here. The room was illuminated only by a large hanging chandelier that resembled a stylized collection of sharp claws, each one as long as her arm, each with an incandescent bulb at its point. There were artful portraits of stern-looking men and women on the walls, perhaps former directors of Black Incorporated. Even in likeness, they projected money and power.

"Is one of those paintings of Mr. Black?" asked Alessandra.

"No," responded Ms. Hammond. "He doesn't need his own face on the wall. And he doesn't like to show off."

"But…"

"I have something for you," Ms. Hammond said to Alessandra. She touched a perfectly manicured finger to Alessandra's lips. Alessandra shuddered at her touch. She wondered what this goddess had in store for her. Perhaps she would lead Alessandra to the sofa and push her gently into those solf fleshy pillows…

But no. Ms. Hammond crossed the room to the desk and rummaged in the top drawer until she found what she was looking for: a large envelope and a single sheet of paper. She held up the envelope as if it were a holy object before placing it on the desk next to the paper and beckoning Alessandra to sit in one of the smaller chairs.

"This is from Mr. Black," said Ms. Hammond. "It's your contract. Read it carefully and sign at the bottom."

Is there no way for me to meet him before signing? Alessandra thought, but did not say. How ridiculous would it be to question this woman, in this office, in this building?

"Do you have any sense of when Mr. Black might wish to meet me?" she asked instead as she sat down gingerly in the chair. The leather was exactly as supple as it looked. Her butt had never been so cradled.

"You will meet him when the time is right," said Ms. Hammond. "His priorities are his own, and are not for us to question. It was my impression that you understood this. In this role, we do not question, we adapt and accommodate. Was my impression of you correct?"

"Oh, yes," Alessandra said quickly. "Of course, Ms. Hammond."

Ms. Hammond smiled. Her teeth were very white. She had an edge of danger, which made her even sexier to Alessandra, if that were even possible. "The single sheet of paper is a non-disclosure agreement. Please sign the NDA before you touch the envelope." She handed Alessandra a silver-and-gold Montblanc fountain pen.

Alessandra scanned the text quickly. "It says here that if I break the agreement, Black Incorporated is entitled to all of my earnings in any job I ever have, for the rest of my life?" *Is that even legal?*

"Yes," Ms. Hammond said with a satisfied smirk, anticipating the question. "It is non-standard, certainly. As for whether it would hold up in court: Mr. Black's relationships within the judiciary in this city are significant. I wouldn't chance it if I were you."

Alessandra tried to ignore the fear that flooded through her. She looked down at the thick white envelope. It was crafted of expensive linen-effect paper and sealed with red wax, stamped with a complex image whose intricacies Alessandra couldn't quite make out. Was that a Latin word? An eye?

This is my chance. If you don't leap, you don't know if you'll fly or fall. And I intend to fly.

She signed the NDA with a flourish. The ink was bright red as arterial blood.

Ms. Hammond smiled. She handed Alessandra a letter opener in the shape of a claw from a holder on the desk that Alessandra recognized as the infamous Tiffany & Co. sterling silver "tin can". Alessandra cracked the seal gently, slid the letter opener across the seal, and took out a several-page document on Black Incorporated letterhead.

"It brings me great pleasure, Alessandra Ironside, to welcome you to our organization," Alessandra read aloud. *"Your role here will be a varied one, and will require a great deal of physical and mental commitment to the best interests of the organization and to the best interests of your direct manager: myself, and on occasion, Ms. Nellie Hammond in my stead."*

"That's right," said Ms. Hammond.

"This role is unusual in its scope. Please read the accompanying contract to ensure that you are sufficiently prepared for the duties and responsibilities of this position."

"Yes, I know what it says," Ms. Hammond said. "I assisted Mr. Black in scoping out the contract to ensure that it included all relevant information. I suspect you will be surprised, but in my estimation, you will also be pleased. Please review it."

Alessandra turned the page.

JOB TITLE: Executive Assistant (Virginal Submissive).

ANNUAL SALARY: $1,200,000 per annum.

"I'm sorry," gawped Alessandra. "Does this say one million, two hundred thousand dollars per year? Are these commas in the right places?

"It does," said Ms. Hammond. "Mr. Black prefers to offer a high level of compensation for those employees he wishes to retain."

Alessandra's eyes grew wider as she read on. There had to be some catch, surely.

By signing the contract, Alessandra would agree to do whatever Tristan Black asked of her without question. She would get on any flight to anywhere in the world at any time, should he wish to have her assistance with any matter. She would be at the office for as many hours as he chose. Her work attire would be his choice, though he would provide her with a corporate Amex to purchase any attire he requested. Her duties would include accompanying Mr. Black on business trips, taking notes, welcoming his guests on occasion when Ms. Hammond was unavailable...

PERSONAL SERVICES

These responsibilities comprise the majority of your employment requirements. They are non-standard, but are a requirement for this position.

As she read on, Alessandra's heart pounded in her ears and in her temples.

Tristan Black would be "the foremost educator in the schooling of [her] sensuality." Alessandra would ensure that her body was in top condition at all times, hairless from the neck down, and dressed in the attire of Mr. Black's preference - which could include "full nudity in any setting of Mr. Black's choice". She would make herself physically available to him for any purpose he chose, at any time. Her virginity would be his to do with what he wanted.

Alessandra shifted in the chair, her fear mingling with arousal.

"Is this what I think it is?" she whispered.

Ms. Hammond's green-gold eyes glittered with amusement. "Surely you're not surprised, Ms. Ironside. Mr. Black thinks that you are a very attractive young woman. He is confident that you will provide an excellent level of service to him, and he is... enthusiastic about your education."

"And this is all... legal?" whispered Alessandra.

"Oh course it is," said Ms. Hammond. "It's a contract."

"May I ask a question?" asked Alessandra slowly, heart hammering in fear.

"Go ahead." Ms. Hammond raised one eyebrow.

"What if... what if there's a day I don't want to do anything physical?" The words came tumbling out in a river of anxiety. "What if I have my period? What if I'm afraid? I mean, I'm sure I will always be available, of course, I don't want to cause any problems for you or Mr. Black. Trust me. I want this."

As Alessandra said the words, she knew it was true. She *did* want this. This was what she had secretly wanted for as long as she could remember. She wanted someone to tell her what to do, and to give her the opportunity and ability to do it.

Ms. Hammond sat back into the wingback chair. Alessandra was suddenly terrified that she'd said too much. Wouldn't she do *anything* for this life? Wasn't that what she'd said? Had she screwed it up forever? How bad could it possibly be?

"Ms. Ironside," said Ms. Hammond gently. "Alessandra. Mr. Black is strict, and he knows what he wants, but this contract is not a license for him or anyone else to harm you. You will not be forced to engage in any activities without your consent. Mr. Black holds enthusiasm as the highest value in these liaisons. It is our expectation that you will make every effort to be enthusiastic in your job performance, and tolerant of some discomfort where requested by Mr. Black. However, he will never do you permanent harm, and you will always have the option to refuse, even if we would prefer you didn't."

"I…" Alessandra stammered.

"Let me put this more clearly for you, my dear," said Ms. Hammond. "Mr. Black has no interest in fucking someone who does not wish for him to do so. He wishes for an assistant who wants to be fucked. Is that you, Alessandra Ironside?"

"I think so," Alessandra squeaked.

Ms. Hammond smiled. "Mr. Black has been watching you for a while. He suspected you would be amenable. Please sign the contract. Once it's signed, we can begin your first-day tasks."

The office was silent except for the scratch of the pen on paper as Alessandra signed her life and her body away to the world's most famous billionaire.

"Beautiful," said Ms. Hammond as Alessandra handed her the signed contract. The gorgeous woman's smile sent a shiver through Alessandra's body. "Mr. Black has asked me to begin with an evaluation for you. He wishes for me to research your physical responses to various stimuli and report back. Why don't you take off those clothes, lie down on the couch, and we'll begin?"

5

"It's normal," said Ms. Hammond as she ran her fingers across the dampness of Alessandra's panties, "to be nervous and aroused at the same time. You'll find that the combination is a common occurrence here. I suggest you learn to enjoy it."

Alessandra could barely breathe. Her D&G skirt suit was hung over the small chair in front of the desk, put there handily by Ms. Hammond so as not to wrinkle it. Now she lay on her back on the couch, her legs spread for Ms. Hammond's examination, and the sexiest woman she'd ever seen was *touching* her.

"Ah, Alessandra. This is good to see. You are *very* swollen. Excellent blood flow."

Ms. Hammond's perfect fingernail dragged gently over the silky fabric that covered her clit. Alessandra nearly jumped at the bolt of pleasure that hit her. She tried to steady her breathing. She didn't think she'd ever been so aroused. Every nerve stood at the ready.

"Excellent response to gentle stimulation, too. I like this." Ms. Hammond's fingers hooked over the top of Alessandra's panties and pulled them down and then off. Alessandra was fully nude now - *full nudity in any setting* - and fully exposed to Ms. Hammond. The office air was cool on the soaked and needy gate to her love-temple. She shivered.

"I'm going to touch you in a few different ways now, Alessandra. This is at Mr. Black's request."

A sudden sharp slap on her right buttock lit up Alessandra's body with burning pain. "Ow!" she cried.

And yet… accompanying the pain was a sharp burst of pleasure alongside it, like two particles in a supercollider on parallel paths.

"That's what I was hoping to see," purred Ms. Hammond. "The dual response. I will take some credit for encouraging Mr. Black to pursue your candidacy. Let's try that again." A slap on Alessandra's left buttock produced a similar response. "Good, good. I think you're ready."

"Ready?" Alessandra breathed.

"For the next step in our discovery process." Ms. Hammond smiled and licked her lips, leaving them glistening even more. "If I'm honest, I've been looking forward to this part of your onboarding for quite some time."

Gently, but with increasing firmness, Ms. Hammond slid two fingers inside Alessandra's pussy, curling them and pressing up on the rough ridges of her G-spot. She moved her fingers gently and rhythmically while Alessandra squirmed and moaned. *Oh, God,* she thought. *If you are truly the king of all Creation, why would you deny your people this pleasure? Why would you tell us this is a sin? How could this be a sin?*

Alessandra watched and trembled as Ms Hammond lowered those gorgeous lips to her pussy and began to lick.

Need. I need this. Ms. Hammond's tongue was slick and quick and skilled. She pursed her lips together over Alessandra's clit and sucked gently as starbursts exploded in Alessandra's brain. There were no thoughts, no emotions, nothing but sheer desperate physical need. Nothing but the delicious gentle drag of Ms. Hammond's tongue over her clit, making firm little circles and then soft ones. Her clit was a toy and Ms. Hammond was at play. Her clit was an instrument and Ms. Hammond was first chair. She brought Alessandra to the edge of oblivion, played with her there for a few moments, and then backed off.

"Please," Alessandra begged, her voice mangled with want. "Oh, God, please, I need it, I need you…"

"Alessandra," Ms. Hammond murmured through her fluid-glazed lips. "This job is not about what you need. It's about what Mr. Black needs. Do you understand?" With that last word came a slap, harder now, across both buttocks.

"Yes," Alessandra mewled. "Yes, I understand."

"You will have satisfaction, to be sure," Ms. Hammond said. She licked Alessandra a few more times, holding her legs apart, as Alessandra squealed and squirmed. God, she was strong. *She must be so muscular under that leather suit.* "But it will not be on your schedule. It will be on Mr. Black's. And, in his absence, when he permits, on mine."

With one finger, Ms. Hammond rubbed Alessandra's clit gently in a slow circle, wetted by her saliva and Alessandra's juices. Again, as Alessandra's breath quickened and she approached the point of no return, Ms. Hammond stopped suddenly. Alessandra groaned in desperation.

"Mr. Black is an unusual figure. He has unusual desires. You may find them strange, even offputting. None of them are dangerous, and none of them are… unsanitary. But they are unconventional. I trust you will be able to handle yourself."

"Yes," Alessandra begged. "Please, I will. Please. I promise."

Ms. Hammond bit her lip. Alessandra's vision was blurry with desire. She could think of very little else other than the fire burning in her clit, in her nipples, across the surface of her skin. Even the hot pain of the slaps had become pleasure in her mind. She needed touch. *Needed* it.

And yet, she would wait until Ms. Hammond wished to touch her. Or Mr. Black.

For what seemed like a million years, Alessandra panted on the couch, dripping from her pussy, incandescent with desire.

"Ms. Ironside," purred Ms. Hammond. "I am pleased at your pleasant scent. And, frankly, your taste is exceptional. I believe we can conclude today's discovery session. There will be more."

Ms. Hammond leaned back down and buried her face between Alessandra's legs. This time, she held back nothing. Her tongue fluttered and dragged and fluttered and dragged against Alessandra's naked clit. She nibbled and sucked, alternating gentle suction with even gentler kisses. And as Alessandra's body tensed in anticipation of orgasm, Ms. Hammond slid three fingers into her pussy and wiggled them deliciously as she sucked her clit firmly between those perfect lips, flickering her tongue across it.

The explosion of her orgasm was like nothing Alessandra had ever experienced. Her entire body clenched, bound with pleasure that set alight every nerve in her body. A waterfall of liquid gushed past Ms. Hammond's lips and splashed onto the couch as Alessandra's cries echoed from the walls of the room.

It could have been a minute or an hour before Alessandra's body slowed its shuddering. She was covered in sweat and her face was bright red. She lay on the couch, all her energy spent, eyes half-closed, in the afterglow of ecstasy.

"I believe Mr. Black will be pleased with his new hire." Ms. Hammond had gone back to the desk and taken something else out from a drawer. "I know you're likely sleepy, but there's no time to rest. There is a door next to the bookcase on the far right; behind it is a shower facility where you can clean up and re-do your hair and makeup. Instead of your current attire, you will wear this."

Ms. Hammond had something in her hand: a bit of white lace peeked out from folded tissue paper.

"What is that?" Alessandra asked softly.

Ms. Hammond handed it to her. The tissue paper, she could see, was printed with *Fleur du Mal* in iridescent letters. Alessandra gaped. This was *very* high-end lingerie.

"That's your uniform for today," Ms. Hammond said. "On normal office days, your skirt suit will suffice. On other days, your office attire will be more in this vein."

Alessandra gaped.

"The contract clearly states that you are required to wear exactly what Mr. Black has requested of you for that day," Ms. Hammond reminded her.

"Of course," breathed Alessandra. "Of course I'll do it."

Inside the tissue paper was a small triangle bralette and a barely-there thong. Even though she had just spent the past half hour lying naked on the couch, Ms. Hammond's head buried between her thighs, she suddenly felt even more exposed, even more embarrassed. *Did I really just do that?*

Alessandra was about to excuse herself to the washroom when Ms. Hammond motioned for her to stay still. "You know, I've changed my mind. I like you when you're messy, and I think Mr. Black will, too. Just put it on here."

Alessandra did as she was told, but Ms. Hammond motioned for her to stop again and made a twirling motion with her finger.

"Turn around," she said. "I want to watch you put them on from behind."

Alessandra turned around slowly. She put on the bralette and then bent over to put one leg, then the other leg through the lacy thong. The fabric tugged deliciously at her still-swollen pleasure boat as she stood.

For what seemed like eternity, Alessandra stood there, staring at the bookcase, wondering what would happen next. For the first time, she noticed the book titles. *The Story of O. Desire and its Interpretation. The Plague of Fantasies. Simulacra and Simulation. Jurassic Park.*

And then she heard the distinctive sound of Ms. Hammond's clicking high heels moving away from her.

"Good work, Ms. Ironside," she said. "You've done well today so far. There is an additional task list on the desk. Depending on how you do with your tasks for the next few hours, you may be meeting Mr. Black in person by this evening."

Alessandra's body swelled with excitement. "Really?"

"As long as as you complete the list provided on the desk," she said. "And again, that all depends on how diligently you work. You must show Mr. Black that you *want* it."

"I want it," said Alessandra.

But Ms. Hammond had already left. The wooden doors clicked shut. Alessandra was completely alone, standing in a pile of her own clothes, naked save for the miniscule scraps of fabric that covered her nipples and crotch. She glanced over at the task list on the desk. The white paper sat there, gleaming like a beacon.

Alessandra walked over to the desk and began to read.

What am I going to be paid a million dollars a year to do? Let's see.

6

The list contained only five items:

1. File this week's reports in alphabetical order. Reports can be found in the second drawer down on the left.

2. Dust each portrait with an approved feather duster, provided in the bottom left drawer of the desk.

3. Reschedule all of Mr. Black's meetings for the next six days.

4. Polish all sterling silver sculptures on the bookcase.

5. Deliver the goat.

Alessandra stopped at the final one. "Deliver the goat?" she said out loud. "That can't be right. What could Tristan Black possibly want with a goat?"

Her mind began to dance with possibilities. Was goat an acronym? GOAT? The "greatest of all time"? Or was it a business term that she was not yet acquainted with?

She looked up at one of the panels behind the desk and, for the first time, saw a camera pointed directly at her.

Her face went hot. Someone had been watching her the whole time. It must have been Mr. Black himself. At least, she hoped it was. Perhaps he was waiting to see how she would react to that little list. Perhaps that was how he would determine his moves with her. Had he watched her entire encounter with Ms. Hammond?

Her face grew hot with embarrassment and deep-seated shame.

And then something in her said *no*. No to shame. No to embarrassment.

For the love of God, she was *enjoying* herself. This felt *right*.

Inspired by a sudden burst of energy from her inner tigress, Alessandra decided to show Tristan Black everything she had. She pictured the freedom she had felt in bed the night before, and the astounding pleasure of her liaison with Ms. Hammond - the heat, the longing, the desire to please and be pleased, the insatiable sexual energy, the being that had always wanted to be unleashed but had never been allowed to.

Moving her body as freely as she would in a strip tease, Alessandra locked eyes with the camera, blew it a kiss, and began her tasks.

She'd figure out the goat at some point.

This is hilarious. Alessandra almost had to laugh. Trying to be sexy while filing paperwork was a unique challenge, though she tried to wiggle her butt as seductively as possible as she bent down.

Next, as she called Mr. Black's associates to reschedule his meetings, she fondled her nipples through the thin scraps of fabric that barely held her breasts; the jolts of pleasure gave a low huskiness to her voice that she hoped the secretaries appreciated.

Polishing and scrubbing was much easier to make enticing. Alessandra took her time with the sculptures, rubbing the tarnished spots with enough vigor to make her breasts bob and jiggle and her round ass shake with the movement of her hips. And, surprisingly, she was having fun. It was freeing to be so naked, to have no need for the restraints of polite society. *I could totally live in a nudist colony,* Alesssandra giggled to herself. *Or a nudist office building. I suppose that's what this is... for me, at least.*

Just as she had finished polishing the Tiffany silver tin can, the wooden doors opened again. Alessandra jolted and covered herself by reflex, but to her relief, it was Ms. Hammond standing at the door.

"Good work today, Ms. Ironside," Ms. Hammond purred through those perfectly skilled lips. "Mr. Black will see you now."

Alessandra could barely contain her excitement. Before she could say anything in response, a bookcase - the one that held *A Plague of Fantasies* - slid open to reveal a doorway. A black curtain hung in its entrance, its velvet texture shimmering.

Alessandra looked expectantly at Ms. Hammond. Ms. Hammond gave her that quirky smile.

"You want me to go in there?" said Alessandra.

"Mr. Black wishes for you to enter," Ms. Hammond purred like a cheetah.

Alessandra moved the black velvet curtain aside and stepped cautiously into the dimly lit room beyond.

The first thing Alessandra saw was the walls, which shone with the most brilliant shade of crimson Alessandra had ever seen. *What Pantone shade is this?* she wondered.

And then she saw the gear.

Tools of leather and metal, large and small, were arrayed on shelves and hung from hooks bolted into the walls. She could only guess at their function. Along the far wall were a few larger contraptions. As her eyes adjusted to the dim light, she saw more and more details. I-hooks with dangling ropes. An entire shelf devoted to whips, and another devoted to paddles. A piece of furniture (?) that looked like a cross between a doctor's examination table and a leather-covered ottoman. A rack of handcuffs in different materials and sizes.

For the first time, Alessandra was truly afraid.

What in the world? What have I gotten myself into?

It was as if she'd gotten a taste of Heaven and then gone straight to Hell. Exactly as Pastor Joseph had warned her.

There was the sudden *click* of an opened lock. The sound of scraping metal echoed through the room, followed by the "click click click" of... footsteps? Claws? Was there a raccoon in here?

There was a loud, bleating
"*MYEHHHHHEHEHEHEH*".

Holy shit. Is that... a goat? The goat?

The goat stepped out from behind the curtain and let out another bellow that echoed against the walls and reverberated deep into her soul.

"*Satan will appear to you, then, you sinners,*" Pastor Joseph boomed in Alessandra's mind, in her memory, as she froze with terror. This had been one of his favourite sermons. "*Satan will appear to you in the form of a great goat, with great horns! The Goat of Hell is clever! His horns are sharp and his appetite endless. He will set upon you with malice and tear you to pieces, body and soul. His hooves will soil you, his horns will desecrate you. Beware the Goat, your eternal soul's doom!*"

Alessandra screamed.

And then, before the beast could call out again, an enormous dark shape leapt from the shadows and devoured the goat in one single gulp.

7

The creature's jaws clamped down hard. The poor goat's blood gushed from its mangled body, spraying across the room in gouts of gore, splashing Alessandra with hematological fluids as if she were a Jackson Pollock canvas in a thong. She watched in Biblical horror as the jaws clamped down again and again, listened to the sick crunch and gelatinous squish of the beast's teeth dismantling the goat's bones and brain and organs until there was nothing left but scraps of fur and viscous, congealing flesh-nuggets.

The creature looked over at Alessandra. He was enormous, at least ten feet tall. His head was long and reptilian, his jaw humongous, his mouth and teeth streaked with the bloody mess of the goat-remnants. His skin - *hide?* - shimmered with a surprising iridescence, as if it was embedded with little sequins. A downy mass of tiny feathers sprouted from his head in a soft ridge, matted and clotted with red-brown goat-blood. His body was powerful, his legs muscled, his arms small and lithe. He stood in an upright crouch like a cross between a salamander and a kangaroo.

Like a…

Dinosaur?

Alessandra gaped. Her mind worked furiously as it all fell into place.

She saw it now. Of course. The public reticence. The rumours. The take-no-prisoners approach to capitalist efficiency. The hostile takeovers. The consistent investment in weapons manufacturers.

This was Tristan Black. The world's most elusive multi-billionaire.

And she had just signed a contract to be his bitch.

Mr. Black's enormous head swiveled towards Alessandra. His saurian eyes glistened. They flashed with a hunger that was primal… but somehow different. The look was carnal. Lustful.

Alessandra, it seemed, would be a meal of an entirely different nature.

"Tristan Black," she whispered.

"Yes, my dear," laughed Ms. Hammond, startling Alessandra as she stepped through the velvet curtain. "This is Tristan Black, your boss. And mine."

"He's a dinosaur," said Alessandra dumbly.

"A Gorgosaur, to be more precise" said Ms. Hammond. "He's a carnivore, so most people in the office are a bit wary of him. Luckily, his ferocious appetite only extends to goats, and sometimes chickens. Occasionally a turkey at Christmastime. And, well..." She looked Alessandra up and down approvingly. "There are his *other* appetites. Those seem to be focused almost entirely on you."

"There was a man on the train..." Alessandra began helplessly.

"That's right! Alberto. He's a lovely specimen, yes. He's in Human Resources. He mentioned he'd seen you on his way home. He was very complimentary. But please don't start getting any ideas about any humans, Alessandra." She smoothed her hair and smiled. "Well, other than me. But as for men? Well, males? Our dear Tristan is your one and only."

Alessandra watched Tristan, who looked back at her with that animalistic gaze. There was something entrancing about him in the power of his jaws, in the way he decimated his prey with absolute hunger. His mouth moved as he continued to chew on a mouthful of ex-goat, and another spurt of blood squirted out between his teeth and hit her directly in the chest, right above her heart.

A frothy, slimy mixture of dinosaur saliva and goat-gristle ran in rivulets down her breast and dripped from her nipple.

Why is this sexy? Why, in God's name, do I want this creature to ram me like a monster truck?

Perhaps it was the goat. The imagery ran deep in her mind.

"The Great Goat," roared Pastor Joseph, in front of a congregation of terrified children and their stern parents. *"Satan will come to you in the guise of a goat. His blood will be thick and hot. His eyes will be of flame and his bones of steel. He is the Mark of the Beast made flesh. And you will be tempted by him. Oh, you will be tempted. His cloven hooves will seem to be flowers, his rough bleating to be angels' song. But he is the Great Goat. He is the Devil, and whomever crushes him will be blessed by God."*

And here was Tristan Black, the saurian billionaire, who had crushed a goat in his jaws.

Alessandra gave her head a small shake. This was insane. *Insane.*

And yet… was it more insane than a culture based on grown men man spit-screaming each Sunday at gathered crowds about an invisible, imperceptible God? A God that would forgive any sin as long as you believed in his Son, but was perfectly happy to discard good people to eternal torment if they believed in a slightly different version? Was it more insane than the concept of God itself? The idea that the world, the universe, was dreamed up by an omnipotent hyperintelligence who was, inexplicably, *very* concerned about the precise length of young women's skirts?

"It's sexy, isn't it?" whispered Ms. Hammond in her ear, the woman's sweet breath tickling Alessandra's skin and making her shiver. "Watching him eat. Knowing that he has the strength to crush any creature in his jaws. There's something… delicious about it."

Alessandra couldn't argue. She had never been so up close with a reptilian carnivore like this. Tristan Black's meat-laden breath was warm and humid even from this distance; it smelled like a bourgeois butcher shop, the kind of high-end meatery that also sold artisan barbecue sauces and was always promising to have Beyond Meat burgers in stock the following week, but never did, but they *would*, one day.

The majesty in Tristan Black's movements was intoxicating. Alessandra was utterly drunk with the carnivorousness of this glorious creature. How was there a dinosaur, living at this moment, this juncture in history? Well – history was full of black-swan events, wasn't it? Surely a universe that delivered a monstrous catastrophe like the extinction of the dinosaurs could also deliver a circumstance in which that extinction hadn't quite been complete, where some uncontacted tribe of hyper-evolved massive saurians could exist. Why the heck not? She'd spent her entire childhood and teenagehood singing compulsory songs about the greatness of God, about His omniscience and His omnipotence. God, the adults in her life always said, could do anything.

So why *couldn't* she have a billionaire dinosaur boss who wanted to fuck her and fly her around the world in luxury?

Fuck you, Pastor Joseph. My God can *do anything.*

Alessandra's panties soddened again. She had a primal attraction to his prowess, to his power both physical and socioeconomic. Even this proximity to power was intoxicating. Being in service to power is itself a kind of power. This was a potent brew indeed, the meaty mist of his goat-laden breath and the knowledge that the building in which he had just fucking crushed that goat was *his*.

Blood dripped from Tristan Black's teeth like rain. And yet when he looked into her eyes, there was no viciousness. She was no prey. There was hunger, certainly, but not for her blood. This was a type of hunger she liked. It was the hunger of the man across from her on the subway, of the countless men she had set aside. Of the men in college she'd lusted over, had but would not allow herself to pursue at all because of her family's judgment of her as impure. No longer was she governed by those expectations.

She was hungry, too. She was a carnivore.

"Go on," said Ms. Hammond, her lips touching Alessandra's ear. "We know you want it."

Alessandra whispered, "I do. I do want it." She looked up at Tristan Black through bowed lashes. "I do," she said loudly and clearly. "I do want you, Tristan."

Tristan looked at her, eyes glimmering with an alien intelligence she struggled to name.

"I'm a virgin," whispered Alessandra. "Well. I've never slept with a man, anyway."

Tristan's expression changed.

Ms. Hammond was silent. For a moment, Alessandra wondered if the woman had mis-sold her to Tristan. But when Alessandra turned around, she saw Ms. Hammond's face suddenly turn sympathetic and kind.

"Don't worry," Ms. Hammond said. "The contract doesn't dictate all aspects of these encounters. He can be gentle... at first."

Tristan Black stalked slowly towards her, the floor creaking under his sheer weight. Alessandra did not move. She quieted the puritanical voice of her parents in her mind, who seemed much less concerned about the fact that she was about to have sex with a dinosaur than they were with the fact that she was about to have sex at all. How absurd it had been to think that her parents should hold any sway over her and her body, which was her own.

Well... contractually, the *use* of her body was Tristan Black's, at least some of the time. But her body itself? That was hers, now and forever. Alessandra stood tall and proud, her body exposed to him entirely. She was ready for whatever came next, truly.

He leaned in close and nuzzled his enormous nose into her hair, taking in every last bit of sweetness the musk of her skin had to offer, pulling her silky strands up into his gaping nostril that emanated meat-scent. She shuddered in anticipation. This was more than any man had made her feel, ever in her life.

Tristan took hold of her gently in his tiny little gorgosaur-arms, which were much stronger than her encyclopedias would have led her to believe. He picked her up off the ground and placed her onto the large leather table-bed-ottoman. Out of the corner of her eye she saw Ms Hammond sink down into a leather-lined papasan chair, her blouse unbuttoned, her breasts exposed as she gently rubbed her dark nipples in anticipation.

You dirty bitch, Ms. Hammond, Alessandra thought with amusement. And with some level of triumph. Ms. Hammond was the most beautiful woman Alessandra had ever seen. She was sleek, she was smart, she was powerful. And yet *Alessandra* was the one the billionaire wanted to fuck.

She was glad Ms. Hammond would be watching, though. She liked the woman. And perhaps watching her reaming by the dino would inspire Ms. Hammond to make a habit of their earlier liaison. She *had* had an extraordinarily talented tongue.

Deftly, somehow, despite his talons, Tristan removed the scrap of thong that still clung to Alessandra's otherwise naked body and guided her legs open. Alessandra shuddered again. The beast above her appeared almost to smile, satisfied with her obedience. She wasn't sure whether the smile had been a mirage, but it had seemed legitimate. Then his head dipped down between her thighs.

Alessandra gasped. The first touch! His tongue was unlike anything else she could imagine, anything else still living. The sensation of his long wide tongue lapping at her clit, licking away at the juices that poured from her like a gushing waterfall, was euphoric. Her breath stopped as her muscles clenched around Tristan's great mouth-muscle, juddered to a start again only when she reminded herself that she must breathe again, taking in every sensation as if it were her last day on earth. As if she were a dinosaur 65 million years ago, but aware that doom was imminent and certain, and she wanted the last sensations of her existence, before the eternal silence swallowed her, to be a beautiful, muscular, nearly prehensile dinosaur tongue licking her clit like an ice-cream cone.

And then she felt it: a tsunami that built inside of her, that shook her undulating hips with tension - the beginning of an orgasm that begged to be released. As if on cue, Tristan began to suck furiously on Alessandra's clit. As her eyes rolled back and her toes clenched, she caught a glimpse of Ms. Hammond cresting her own wave of ecstasy, watching them through half-lidded eyes, her finger teasing her own clit as she slid three fingers from her other hand in and out of her pussy.

Just as the tsunami had built to an impossible tension, it released its fury. Her orgasm quaked with such power that she feared she would drown in pleasure, goodbye, never coming back from this paradise. Tristan took all of it with glee, lapping at her pussy until the quaking had ceased and his paramour laid motionless below him.

Alessandra's eyelids fluttered as she stared at Tristan Black, the famous billionaire, the object of her desire, the fantastic beast who had taken her where no man ever had. She wanted nothing more but to stay in that moment for the rest of time, to lay on that mutant table-ottoman in that crimson room full of perplexing but strangely appealing equipment with Tristan Black as her silent sexy sentinel until the sun rose the next day.

"Job well done, Ms. Ironside," came the languid voice of Ms. Hammond from the corner.

And an answering sound from Tristan: a strangely birdlike growl-chirp that was sexy as hell.

With a smile on her lips, Alessandra closed her eyes and drifted off to sleep.

8

The morning light against her skin gently brought Alessandra to wakefulness. She was back home, in her own room at her apartment.

She looked around, confused. *Was it all just a dream?*

Everything around her was exactly as it would have been if she'd just passed out after a long day at work. Her work clothes were folded on her chair. Her morning face routine was all assembled at the bathroom sink, which she could see through the half-open bathroom door. Her alarm was set, though she'd woken up before it. Everything looked perfectly normal.

Am I literally going crazy?

And then her phone rang. The caller ID said MS N HAMMOND.

She stared at the phone for a moment, not knowing what she should say. *Hi, Ms. Hammond. How did you get into my apartment? How did I not wake up? Does my billionaire dinosaur boss secrete some kind of weird soporific drug in his saliva? Do you? Also, what the literal actual fuck was yesterday?*

She pushed the green button. "Hello?" she said tentatively.

"How did you sleep?" purred the voice on the other end.

I guess it wasn't a dream. I'm actually the hired fucktoy of a literal billionaire literal dinosaur and his ridiculously sexy assistant. Cool cool cool.

"I slept very well," she finally responded. "Yesterday was a strange day."

"But you enjoyed it?" asked Ms. Hammond, with confidence.

"I did," said Alessandra.

There was a long pause on the other end. For a moment, Alessandra wondered if Ms. Hammond had hung up. But the sound of a coffee grinder in the background let her know the gorgeous woman was still there.

"We'll be meeting offsite this morning," said Ms. Hammond. "Well, semi-offsite. When you arrive at Black Incorporated today, ask to be taken to the cafe. They'll know where to escort you. Your presence is required at 9 AM sharp, so please don't be late."

Before she could ask any more questions, Ms. Hammond had hung up.

Alessandra put down the phone and stared out her window at her familiar view: a chunk of the next building over, a half-bald patch of grass, and the motley collection of garbage bins that hulked stinking at the back of the building, waiting to be emptied. It was a far cry from the opulent luxury of her new office space at Black Incorporated... or Tristan Black's office space.

Once her first paycheque came through - a paycheque for *fifty thousand dollars for two weeks' work* - she'd have enough money to get a new apartment. Hell, she'd be able to put a down payment on a condo of her very own. No more paying rent. No more view of the garbage bins. A life of luxury would be hers.

But if day one was that crazy... how much crazier could it get?

What could be the reason for an offsite meeting? Something in Ms. Hammond's tone made Alessandra wonder what kinds of lusty insanity were in store for her today.

Her thoughts drifted back to Tristan Black. His eyes that glittered and glowed in the dim light of the red room. The rough-smooth-downy scaled skin that caressed her open thighs as his gargantuan body loomed above her. The huge prehensile tongue that had lapped so fervently at her soaked and dripping love-tunnel gate, the heat and hunger from him that had flowed through her body like lava and erupted into an orgasm that felt volcanic…

Alessandra swung her legs over the side of the bed, padded to her closet and opened the door. She knew that Tristan Black would probably dress her in some skimpy lingerie, but she wanted to start the day off right, too. She pulled out something that she had not worn since her university days: a tight red bandage dress, an H&M knockoff of Herve Léger that looked far more expensive than it was. She added a long structured black blazer over it in case it needed to be more business-appropriate at the beginning.

Perfect. Business on top, party underneath.

And with that, Alessandra laid the dress on her bed and made her way to the shower, to scrub and shave and preen and make herself into Mr. Black's most incredible confection.

Alessandra arrived at 8:50 AM. When she asked at
reception to be taken to "the cafe", the young man behind the
desk gave her a quizzical look, but his colleague, an older
man with a magnificent grey moustache, piped up. "Yes,
I've been instructed. Please follow me."

The man took her in the elevator down to the third
basement level and through a small maze of tunnels.
Throughout their journey he was mostly silent, giving one-
word answers to Alessandra's attempts at making
conversation, but not rudely – he seemed instead to be
singularly focused on the journey. Eventually, a door at the
end of a hallway led into a small cafe, brightly illuminated
by the sun streaming in from a huge skylight.

Ms. Hammond was already there, and she was
dressed for the occasion. She wore her hair down, flowing
past her shoulders, her glasses perched on the end of her
lovely straight nose as she perused the menu. A black form-
fitting dress graced her body, the plunging neckline
accentuating her perfect breasts. Most of the other tables
were populated by men in nice suits, and they were all either
looking at Ms. Hammond or trying their best not to.

Ms. Hammond looked up at Alessandra and smiled.

Alessandra took off the blazer and hung it over her
arm, and strode across the floor as each pair of male eyes

fixated upon her, on the tight red dress with the skirt that barely touched the middle of her thighs and the high-heeled black boots that clicked across the floor with absolute confidence. She felt like a queen: her inner tigress had finally come out to play without shame. When she joined Ms. Hammond at the table, she could sense the awe of the men surrounding them, the deep admiration of their bodies and the animalistic lust. But Ms. Hammond and Alessandra weren't for them. These men could look, but not touch.

"Well, look at you," said Ms. Hammond with a brilliant smile. "You look like a whole new woman."

"I feel like one," said Alessandra. "Thanks to you. For a while, I wondered if yesterday was a dream."

Ms. Hammond took a sip of the coffee beside her. "That's normal. It's hard to believe when you see him for the first time. But when you do…"

"…it's incredible," said Alessandra, more dreamily than she'd intended.

"Yes. Now you know why we've been so adamant about finding the right person. But if you read the contract fully, you'd know that this is only the beginning."

"I did read it, of course." *Full submission. One point two million dollars per year.*

"Yes. As you can probably tell, Tristan has some... distinctive tastes. We outlined it all in the contract, but as you were a..." At this moment, Ms. Hammond lowered her voice. "A virgin. Because you were a virgin, we knew that jumping straight into the... apparatus... would be too much. We had to soften you up. But we both agree now that you seem ready. You seem to have a naughty side that is very appealing to both of us."

The inner tigress. Was it possible that Ms. Hammond could sense her presence? Alessandra smiled and looked down at the table, trying but failing to hide the heady fear-lust mixture that rose in her.

"I've always thought I would enjoy something like this," she said. "To be honest, the fact that I wasn't supposed to think that way for so long made it even more exciting for me."

"Then you know what's in the contract? You did read it over?"

Alessandra nodded. "I mean, of course. I would never sign anything without reading it fully."

Ms. Hammond seemed to be caught off guard. "Does it shock you that I read it all?" asked Alessandra.

Ms. Hammond smiled. "Maybe. Or maybe it still surprises me that you aren't perturbed by all that will be required of you. I'm not sure why I'm surprised, after yesterday." The gorgeous woman reached out and touched Alessandra's thigh under the table, which sent a jolt of sex-electricity through her. "It was *very* good to get to know you. I think we've just been searching for the right person for so long that I can't quite believe we have her."

"I've lived a sheltered life, Ms. Hammond," confessed Alessandra. "At least, until recently. My parents were church people. *Are* church people. I went to a private church school and my only activity outside of school was our church youth group. I was raised with the notion that purity and chastity were the most important qualities for any young woman to possess."

Ms. Hammond nodded along, sympathetic.

"But even though I went along with it, and maybe I even believed in it a little bit," continued Alessandra, "I went away to college because I knew that there was a whole big world out there. And although my childhood trauma kept me virginal until now, I've slowly been coming around to a truth that's central to my entire being-in-the-world, that I'd kept secret even from myself for so long that it had almost been lost. But now it's found."

"And what truth is that, Ms. Ironside?" Ms. Hammond whispered, sultry.

"Well, Ms. Hammond. The truth is that I've always wanted to be fucked hard and rough by someone who could handle me."

Ms. Hammond's smile widened. Alessandra looked around to see that all the men in the restaurant were staring at them. Had they all heard the women's conversation? Had these men actually been listening to women talking?

The men in the room, all of them in beautiful business suits, all of them perfectly groomed and perfectly proper, were staring at the pair with all the hunger and lust that she had seen in Tristan the night before, with an addictive combination of lust, admiration and desire.

It was intoxicating to Alessandra.

"Do you think they heard me?" she whispered with a wry grin that she hoped was much like Ms. Hammond's.

"Perhaps," said Ms. Hammond. "But I think it's your aura they're noticing. You have that glow about you now. That temptress edge. There's a new light in you, Alessandra, and I think you know that as you continue in your employment with us, your ongoing delight in the delicious pleasures of this role will only enhance your natural appeal. It's hard not to notice that."

A man across the room stared at Alessandra with the lustful eyes of a satyr in a Renaissance painting. He was dark and handsome, his perfectly coiffed hair and perfectly turned out suit - was it Prada? Tom Ford? - lending him his own aura. Power, money, privilege. No one said no to this man.

He made a motion to the young female server who stood beside him. The server leaned towards him and he whispered into her ear; she nodded as the handsome man kept his eyes locked on Alessandra. After a brief conversation, the server approached Ms. Hammond and Alessandra's table.

"Excuse me, ladies," said the server. "The man across the restaurant would like to buy you both drinks."

Ms. Hammond put up her hand and shook her head to the server.

"Please thank him for his kind offer," she said with a brilliant smile. "But this young lady is the property of Mr. Black, and we cannot allow that."

Property of Mr. Black. Alessandra was almost disturbed at how good it felt to hear that.

The rest of the day was so ordinary that, by afternoon, Alessandra began to question whether everything that had happened was a mirage. Sitting in "her" office, looking out over the city, her work was like any other office job: she took calls, answered emails, filed paperwork, made lists.

Of course, she wore the red dress, which reminded her that this was very much *not* an ordinary office job.

Every once in a while, she saw Ms. Hammond looking over at her from an adjacent office, her expression both satisfied and intrigued.

At five o'clock, Ms. Hammond fetched Alessandra and led them both into Tristan Black's office. "I ordered sushi for us," she said. "I trust you like it. Or that you'll learn to like it. It's my favourite."

"Of course," said Alessandra.

They feasted in silence. The day of silent flirting had made Alessandra a little nervous, despite the delights of the previous day. Ms. Hammond was obviously a skilled and practiced lover of women, and although Alessandra had been out of her mind with pleasure at the beauty's ministrations, she wasn't nearly as confident in her own potential. And there was also a sick worry at the bottom of her stomach:

what if she enjoyed taking it, but couldn't dish it out? What if she just didn't like giving?

I'll learn, I suppose.

Ms. Hammond looked up, giving Alessandra an incredibly sexy smile. "You seem nervous. Are you nervous?" she asked.

Alessandra blushed. "Maybe a little bit. You're so... good. And I've never been with a woman other than you, and I'm just not sure if I'll be good, too. I'm a little afraid I'll disappoint you, and..."

Before she could finish her sentence, Ms. Hammond leaned forward and kissed her softly.

Any doubts in Alessandra's mind floated away like helium balloons over the horizon as she lost herself in the sweet, sensual touch of Ms. Hammond's lips. She felt Ms. Hammond's tongue press into her mouth and she melted into her. This was ecstasy. *This.* This was what she wanted. The inner tigress roared. Every bit of fear or nervousness, every catastrophizing impulse, dissolved into the delicious taste of her mentor's mouth.

After a long, beautiful, languid kiss, Ms. Hammond pulled away. She looked deep into Alessandra's eyes with her own enormous green-gold ones. Alessandra was so close that she could see the tiny muscles of the woman's iris moving, opening her pupils to take her in even more.

"It's time," Ms. Hammond whispered.

"Time?" Alessandra's voice was husky and urgent.

Ms. Hammond took Alessandra by the hand and led her towards the curtain to the red room where she had her encounter with Tristan Black the night before.

This is really happening. Again.

Anticipation clawed at her from inside her ribcage, arcing out to every sensual point on her body. Alessandra could barely walk. Her legs felt watery and unsteady. All she wanted out of life was to lie on that strange furniture, open the gates between her legs, and drown this woman and this dinosaur in the fluids that ran like a spring river out of her body.

The lights of the red room were dimmed yet strangely luminous. Candles had been lit all around the room, wax dripping from golden candelabras and pooling on circular tables beneath them. The air was thick with excitement and lust.

There was something new today: a long, plush leather settee, several times the width of a normal piece of furniture, as if Ms. Hammond had bought it on Facebook Marketplace from a couple of giants.

It kind of IS furniture for giants.

Ms. Hammond took Alessandra's hand and led her to the settee. She paused before it, her index finger gently caressing the inside of Alessandra's wrist, raising goosebumps on her arm.

"This is the point of no return," said Ms. Hammond. "If you agree to this, you are putting your body entirely in our hands. Do you understand?"

In a whisper, Alessandra asked: "Will you hurt me? Will you kill me?"

The peal of laughter that burst from Ms. Hammond was so sudden and surprising that Alessandra jumped. "Oh, good lord, my dear, no. You won't be harmed. You certainly won't be killed. In fact, Mr. Black has hired security to ensure your safety at all times. He is very, very taken with you. As am I."

"Really?" Alessandra's heart leaped. *Security. Safety.* She would be safe. It was as if a huge and complicated knot deep inside her, that had been present since she was a child, had just been released.

"Really. As for *hurt*... well, we find that a certain amount of pain acts as seasoning to pleasure. Like salt. But we will never harm you, and any pain we inflict is minor, and always in the service of greater heights of ecstasy. Like those slaps on your backside yesterday. You enjoyed those, yes?"

Alessandra felt an internal juicy gush at the memory. "Oh, yes. I loved them."

"Think that, but more deliberate as an... adjuvant to your pleasure, shall we say."

"In that case..." Alessandra took a deep breath. "In that case, yes. I agree."

"What's about to happen to you will be lifechanging. Once you've experienced these earthly pleasures, you may never again be satisfied with an ordinary human. Tell me one more time. Are you certain?"

"I'm certain," said Alessandra.

At this, Ms. Hammond paused. "It's going to be intense. You'll have... an audience. Are you still certain?"

Alessandra leaned forward and kissed Ms. Hammond again, hungrily, letting her *yes* be known with her body.

Ms. Hammond pulled back and smiled.

"Good. Now we can begin," she said.

9

Before Alessandra knew what was happening, Ms. Hammond had reached out and begun to undress her. She removed Alessandra's boots, then her dress, then her tiny thong, as if she were preparing to devour every part of her.

Once Alessandra was fully nude, Ms. Hammond pushed her down onto her back on the leather settee. The beautiful woman stepped over to a hanging rack and returned with a set of soft leather cuffs for Alessandra's wrists and a set for her ankles, binding her in a vulnerable position. Alessandra gasped. Her legs were bound apart; her pussy was completely exposed, and completely open for whomever wished to see or touch it.

"Trust us," said Ms. Hammond. "You're safe. And you're ready."

Ms. Hammond again leaned forward to kiss her passionately. *RIP this leather,* thought Alessandra as her juices began to flow. To her delight, Ms. Hammond began to undress herself above her. The woman's elegant black dress fell to the floor to reveal a body that must have beel sculpted by God, or at least one of God's senior angels. Her skin was soft and unblemished, with the finest downy hairs. Her figure was lush: wide graceful hips, a nipped-in waist with a Pilates-strong core, the perfect grapelike globes of her breasts. She shone in the candlelight like some divine creature on shore leave from Heaven.

Alessandra grew wetter. She hungered for the delectable meal that had been set in front of her. Her inner tigress roared and rattled the cuffs that held her down, as if in protest of being confronted with such perfect beauty and bound away from it.

Shhhhhh, tigress. You'll have your meal soon.

She got her wish almost immediately. Ms. Hammond moved on top of her and pressed her own wet pussy against Alessandra's open mouth.

Alessandra was almost surprised to find that the process was almost second nature. She needn't have worried about her ability to please this gorgeous creature, it seemed. Alessandra lapped at Ms. Hammond's pussy exactly as the woman had done to her, stroking the entirety of her sex with her tongue as if her open love-portal was a delicious pussy-flavoured soft-serve ice cream. She tasted of musk and tang and a strong yet delicate femininity. *How could I have ever worried that I would hate this?*

Alessandra nibbled on her labia, inner and outer, avoiding her clit as a tease... and then tongued slow circles around Ms. Hammond's ecstasy-button, making her gasp and moan.

Ms. Hammond began to ride her face harder as her legs began to shake. It was then that Alessandra heard a growl: the birdish yet coarse, distinctive growl of the great gorgosaur known as Tristan Black.

He's been watching us this entire time, thought Alessandra. Her love-flower released more of its fragrant nectar onto the long-suffering leather of the settee as she imagined the beast's hunger, what it must feel like for him to have such a carnal meal awaiting him.

As Alessandra continued to explore Ms. Hammond with her tongue, she felt the distinct sensation of rough-smooth dinosaur hide rubbing against her thighs, and the tiny acupunctural pinpricks of talons gently grasping her legs to hold them apart even more. Alessandra gasped against Ms. Hammond's crotch. The cool intake of her breath tipped Ms. Hammond over the edge into a screaming, shaking orgasm that released a pumpkin spice latte's worth of delicious juices into Alessandra's mouth and across her face.

As she gulped down Ms. Hammond's release, Alessandra felt the shaft of Tristan's enormous cock thrust inside of her.

It was *huge*. His dino-penis must hae been at least a foot long and the width of a soda can. She had never known such ecstasy. Her entire vagina was *full* in a way she had never imagined possible without the help of a comically large dildo. But this wasn't a dildo. This was an all-natural, in-the-flesh, prehistoric-but-apparently-not, ribbed-for-her-pleasure-and-also-probably-for-evolutionary-reasons reptilian cock that belonged to a billionaire who was paying her more than a million dollars a year to bring her to ecstatic heights that she hadn't known existed.

"I love my job," whispered Alessandra around her mouthful of Ms. Hammond.

Ms. Hammond, it seemed, wasn't finished having orgasms. She moaned loudly, grinding harder onto Alessandra's eager tongue as Tristan fucked Alessandra - slowly at first, then harder and faster, pounding her tight pussy with the force of a hundred million years of evolution.

And, indeed, Alessandra *loved* it. Every thrust inside her, every thrust above her, the greediness and hunger of the tigress.

With a groan that seemed to be ripped from her soul, Ms. Hammond shuddered to another orgasm, her pussy contracting around Alessandra's chin as her tongue lashed the woman's clit, slowly coming to a stop as Ms. Hammond slumped on top of her in post-orgasmic languor. Finally, she moved off of Alessandra's face, collapsing in the afterglow onto a blanket that lay on the floor next to the settee... only to be replaced with a human cock that bumped at Alessandra's half-open mouth, testicles resting on her chin.

Alessandra startled and closed her lips. "Hmmmmm?" she asked, anxiously looking for the source of the rogue cock. A beautifully sculpted male torso seemed to loom above her, but she couldn't see his face.

"Alberto from HR," Ms. Hammond half-moaned from her comfy spot on the floor. "Mr. Black saw that you'd enjoyed thinking about him on the train, and your pleasure brings him pleasure, so he decided to give you a little present."

Alessandra's heart pounded with joy. Could it be true? Could her boss truly be so kind as to allow her to sample *all* the different possibilities of her erotic fantasies?

Alessandra opened her mouth wide and took the length of the cock down her throat, sucking it with enthusiasm. It tasted different from Ms. Hammond, saltier and less tangy, but no less delicious. She heard a ragged male groan from above her and sucked with even more vigour, using her tongue to press up and down the shaft.

Tristan Black continued to pound her pussy with his giant cock, watching Alessandra in her debauched ecstasy.

The human man suddenly stopped and moved away from her face. Alessandra cried out in disappointment - but then saw that he and Tristan were switching places. Tristan straddled the wide settee with his enormous legs, let out another growl, and thrust his shaft - dripping with her own juices - into Alessandra's mouth. Alessandra gleefully accepted this huge saurian gift. Despite its massive size, she endeavored to take as much of it in her mouth as she could. Initially, she gagged on its length, but Tristan noticed her distress and backed off, giving her exactly as much as she could handle.

There was a chorus of gasps and a few anticipatory moans. Alexandra craned her eyes up. Beyond the scaled body of her dinosaur lover-boss stood at least a dozen others: men and women in expensive suits, staring with eagerness and envy at the spectacle unfolding before them.

An audience. Of course.

"They're all waiting to see if you wish to include them," said Ms. Hammond languidly. "You can dismiss the ones you don't want. Once each one is satisfied, Tristan will take what's his. He wants to save the best part for last…"

"Mmmph," said Alessandra around a mouthful of Tristan, her pussy occupied with the slow-building ecstasy of Alberto's cock-ministrations.

Tristan paused and removed his cock from her mouth. He sat back, giving her an expectant glance.

"I want them all," Alessandra whispered, her sex muscles clenching.

She couldn't be sure, but it seemed as though the dinosaur smiled.

"Good girl," breathed Ms. Hammond.

Whether it was hours or days, it was impossible to tell: for however long, Alessandra lived in a haze of erotic delight. One by one, each beautiful figure in an expensive business suit came forward to take their turn in using Alessandra as their own personal fucktoy. She had never known such surrender, such glorious and perfect bliss. Each cunt that she licked tasted like the sweet nectar of a paradisical flower. Each cock was a rocket that blasted her into sexual heaven. Her own pussy was a spring of eternal lust, of endless slick juices that coated each cock with a thin layer of perfect delight and met each scissoring slit as a constant friend. The hands that groped her and the mouths that feasted on her naked body were her wildest dreams come to life. With every lick and every thrust, Alessandra felt more alive than she ever had.

And through it all, Tristan was there. Occasionally, he watched, but often he returned to explore her body himself. When he did, the others parted like the Red Sea, to let their prophet through.

There was a lull, after a long while. Ms. Hammond had risen from her place on a blanket, and was nowhere to be seen. Alessandra looked around the room to see a dozen nude and half-nude people resting, beautiful in their exhausted satisfaction. She moaned with the absence of cock or cunt. *Could it be over so soon?*

And then, from the corner of her eye, she saw Ms. Hammond approach the settee with another goat.

With one quick slice, Ms. Hammond slit the goat's carotid artery. Blood poured forth from the creature's neck and splattered onto Alessandra. That was, it seemed, Tristan Black's cue.

Tristan took one gargantuan bite from the goat's flesh, soaked his cock in the creature's arterial blood, and mounted Alessandra again, this time positioning his shaft at the entrance to her ass.

A deep groan was all Alessandra could muster as Tristan's cock entered her tight asshole, thrusting in and out with all of the euphoria of a creature in heat.

Where she had expected a ripping pain, there was only pleasure. And this pleasure went *deep*.

The blood from the goat continued to drip onto the settee, which was now in such a state that Alessandra couldn't even imagine the cleaning bill. It would be *thousands*.

Tristan took another bite of the goat in between his thrusts, pounding Alessandra's ass with dinosaur glee as blood splattered around them. The company watched hungrily. Ms. Hammond crawled toward the settee again, her hand reaching between Alessandra's legs. Then, with the greatest skill imaginable, she began to rub Alessandra's clit.

Ms. Hammond's fingers worked swiftly and deftly. The sweet pressure inside Alessandra's ass combined with the sharp delight of her mentor's manipulations of her clit to bring her to the brink almost instantly.

There was a scream of mind-bending bliss as a hurricane of an orgasm ripped through her, at the exact moment when Tristan Black finished inside of her, gouting his reptilian dino-semen into the depths of her colon as her muscles clenched and pulsed around him.

Slowly, he pulled his cock out of her ass. He watched as Alessandra lay motionless, exhausted by ecstasy, covered in the blood and cum and sweat of the people that surrounded her.

Alessandra, for her part, gave a weary smile, her eyes closed. Perhaps she had died and made her way to the gates of Heaven. Perhaps this was all a vision produced by her brain in her final moments of life.

Or perhaps this was her new reality, this life of hedonistic pleasure that never ended.

Thank you, God, for this bounty you have bestowed upon me. Amen.

When she finally opened her eyes, the rest of the men and women were gone. Only Ms. Hammond and Tristan remained. Ms. Hammond held her gently, stroking her hair with the greatest of care, as the . She looked over at Ms. Hammond and smiled again.

"Thank you, Ms. Hammond," she whispered, her tone rapturous.

"Please," said the most beautiful woman in the world, with a perfect smile. "Call me Nellie."

10

When the morning light finally lit up the glistening towers of Black Incorporated, Alessandra was still asleep on a huge couch that had somehow been moved into "her" office in her absence.

She awoke with the knowledge that she had everything she'd always dreamed of. The delights of the previous day still danced in her mind. For a long time, she'd dreamed of a world that held no bounds, where she could be her true self: a treasured, beloved fucktoy. And where she had once come to look for a career as an office worker, she had found herself in a position that could not have been more perfect for her – or for the inner tigress. Before this, the tigress had slumbered for so long that she had almost forgotten her roar. Now, with all that she had experienced, she finally knew what real freedom was... and that there would be no going back.

The morning light slanted through the highrise windows with a heavenly glow. As her eyes adjusted to everything around her, Alessandra realized that her day had already been set up for her. A fresh set of clothes – a low-cut button-up blouse and short pencil skirt – were laid out over the back of her office chair. On a table close by was a fresh cup of coffee.

Alessandra rose gingerly, anticipating soreness from the day before. To her shock, she felt as good as new. *Was I really that wet? I suppose I'll take the win.*

She slowly got dressed and sat in her office chair, crossing her legs, and sipped on her coffee. She knew she should by all rights be exhausted, but she wasn't. She felt ready to work. Whatever Tristan wanted, she would happily do, whenever and wherever he liked it. And Ms. Hammond, too. *Nellie.*

She felt her heart flutter at the thought of having the two of them in her life from now on.

Could I be… falling for him? For them? For both of them?

She was eager to see Tristan Black, her perfect delicious hunk of prehistoric sexiness. The pleasure he had brought her was beyond imagining. Sure, he couldn't speak. But silence and mystery were part of his charm. She wanted to spend more time in his delicious presence, this handsome beast of hers. And besides, who could argue with falling for a multi-billionaire philanthropist? Whatever species he might be? That would be… speciesist.

And then there was Ms. Hammond. *Nellie.* The world's most beautiful woman, the human embodiment of sex, with a pussy like honey and kisses like sweet wine and a body that exemplified the Platonic ideal of femininity.

Both of them had her heart, she realized.

As if summoned by her sudden insight, Ms. Hammond opened the door and walked into the office. She smiled kindly at Alessandra with a softness that was new. She walked over to Alessandra, taking a moment to fix the younger woman's collar with precise care.

"How did you sleep?" she asked coyly.

Alessandra smiled shyly and took a sip of her coffee. "Like I'd died and gone to Heaven, Ms. Hammond," she said.

"Nellie," purred Ms. Hammond. "You can call me Nellie from now on."

Alessandra beamed.

"I can't stop thinking about him," said Alessandra. "Tristan. I know it's not logical, of course. But at the same time, it makes perfect sense to me. There's just... something about him. The way he's made all my fantasies come true as if he knew exactly what I wanted without my even telling him. The way his presence just… calms me and makes me feel safe. It's intoxicating."

"It is," said Nellie. "And he is so enamored of you, Alessandra. He told me this morning before he headed out to his meetings."

Alessandra's heart leapt in delight. "Really? Do you mean that? He said that?!"

Nellie nodded. "He's tried women in your position before, but none have ever made him feel so alive. He wants to see you again tonight. But this time, he wants it to be just the two of you."

Alessandra smiled so hard her face hurt. Her well-used pussy clenched in anticipation of even more delight. "Of course!" she said quickly, urgently. "Whatever he wants! I am his, whenever he wants me, however he wants me. How could I ever do anything else? Oh, gosh, do I need something new to wear?"

"Don't worry about that. He bought you something for the occasion. I'll bring it to you at the end of the day."

Alessandra was in pure bliss, body and soul. Without thinking, she wrapped her arms around Nellie, holding her in a tight embrace.

"Alright, lover girl, settle down," laughed Nellie. "We still have a full day of work to get through."

Ah, yes, Alessandra had almost forgotten about the office work. She turned away to look at the task list for the day on the desk when there was a knock at the door.

"Are you expecting anyone?" Nellie asked, perplexed.

Alessandra shook her head, confused. "No, not at all. I haven't even told anyone yet that I got the job. I have no idea."

Nellie opened the door to a young man who Alessandra vaguely recognized from the night before. He looked concerned, almost frightened. The atmosphere of the room shifted.

"Ms. Hammond," he said. "There is a gentleman here to see you and Ms. Ironside,"

Nellie frowned. "A gentleman? Who is he?"

The man shook his head. "He didn't say?"

"Well then, what does he want?"

"He didn't tell me. All he said was that it was of the utmost importance."

Nellie looked at Alessandra, then back at the young man. Without another word, Alessandra and Nellie walked after him, down the brightly lit hallway towards the reception area for the floor. A feeling of overwhelming dread crept up on Alessandra, so powerful that she was nearly incapable of swallowing it down. Why did she feel this way? She couldn't figure it out, but the closer she came to the front desk, the deeper and darker the sensation grew.

Nellie, on the other hand, seemed terribly impatient. "I hope this doesn't take long," she muttered under her breath as they turned the corner to where the receptionist sat in a large rotunda behind a marble-and-stone desk.

A tall, handsome man stood beside the desk with a sneer.

Alessandra's heart sank. The man, who had been looking down the hallway in anticipation of her arrival, raised his eyebrows at the sight of Alessandra. His eyes crept across her body, taking in her sexpot outfit. Alessandra shuddered and tried to avert her eyes, but the man's steel-cold gaze, followed her, his eyes full of cruelty, amusement and lust.

"Wow," said the man. "That's quite the outfit, Allie."

"Don't you *dare* call me that," Alessandra hissed.

"Too bad you couldn't have dressed like that when we were together."

"We *weren't...*"

"Alessandra, do you know this man?" Nellie interrupted her.

The man laughed and took a step forward, his smile twisted and nasty.

"Of course she does," he said. "I'm her boyfriend."

11

For a moment, all was silent.

"Boyfriend?" Nellie finally whispered, her voice strangled with fear and anger. *"Boyfriend?!"*

"He's not my boyfriend," Alessandra pleaded. "He *wishes*. He just can't let me go. He can't take no for an answer."

The man scoffed and threw his coat over a nearby chair. "Sure, Allie. I'll believe that once you get the rest of your stuff from my condo."

"You told me…" began Nellie.

"She told you she didn't have a boyfriend? Yeah, that's rich. She probably neglected to mention how long we'd been together, too. Two years for nothing."

"We were *not* together!" cried Alessandra. "I stayed at your condo because I had nowhere else to go! You let me sleep on your *couch!*"

"Two years..." mused Nellie, holding up her hand to Alessandra.

The man sighed and plunked his tall bulk down on one of the fine leather chairs arranged in a half-moon in the reception area. "Two long, disastrous years," he continued. "That's not fair - I'm being dramatic. There were a lot of good times, enough to keep us going, or so I thought. Could have been more sex, but women are fickle that way. I get it."

"More sex?" Nellie said, incredulous. She turned to Alessandra. "You told me you were a virgin."

"I am! Well, I *was!*" cried Alessandra. "I didn't sleep with Kyle, I promise. I never even kissed him. I was homeless and afraid, and I knew him from college, and he let me sleep on his couch for a while. That's all. I swear to you, I swear on my life..."

"For two years?" Kyle laughed menacingly. "Who would let a pretty girl sleep on his couch for two years without fucking him?"

"Kyle, what the..."

"I have proof," said Kyle, interrupting her. He took out his phone and began to scroll. "There's a video of this chick taking her clothes off for me. Here," he shoved his phone in Nellie's face, "look."

Nellie watched, and Alessandra watched over her shoulder. It was Alessandra, all right, wearing a slinky bias-cut satin dress she'd found on sale at Zara, facing the camera, the door to the bathroom behind her. She blew a kiss at the camera as she slowly slid one thin strap and then the other off her shoulders, then pulled them down, revealing her beautiful breasts…

Nellie turned to Alessandra, her face a storm. "What is the meaning of this, Ms. Ironside?"

"I don't know!" Alessandra begged. "Maybe he hid a camera in the bathroom mirror? I didn't undress for him. I promise. I *never* let him see me naked. I tried so hard to find somewhere else to stay, but I couldn't find work, and everywhere was so expensive, and my family wouldn't help me because I went to college, and he was my only option…"

Alessandra trailed off. Nellie and the receptionist stared at her, as did a few other men in suits who'd heard the commotion and emerged from their offices to see what the trouble was.

Kyle grinned maliciously. "You think they're actually gonna believe that bullshit story?" he laughed. "Come on, Allie. Let's get you home. You obviously need me to take you shopping for more appropriate clothes. Is this what you wore to your job interviews at all those jobs you tried to get? No wonder you had to "sleep on my couch", and by my couch I mean my cock, for two years. How unprofessional can you be?"

Alessandra was speechless with rage. She opened her mouth to speak, but found she couldn't make a sound, only a strangled sob.

"That's right, you little slut. Come on. I'm taking you home to teach you a lesson."

Alessandra looked pleadingly at Nellie. The beautiful woman looked back at her, stone-faced.

"Nellie, you have to believe me," Alessandra pleaded. "I was a virgin. I'd never been with anyone. Kyle saved me from homelessness, and he got angry when I rejected him. I don't know why he's doing this. Why?" she cried to Kyle. "Why are you doing this? Why are you lying and trying to ruin my life?"

"There's only one liar here, sweetheart," said Kyle, "and it ain't me."

Alessandra wanted to run. Everything in her life, everything she thought she'd found, was crashing down around her, and she didn't know how to stop it.

She'd met Kyle during senior year at a student affairs mixer her roommate had dragged her to. They'd chatted for a while. He'd done a dual degree in math and business, and already had offers from a few of the big consulting firms in the big city. He'd given her his number and told her to look him up if she ever moved downtown. He was handsome, sure, and he was smart, but there was something off-putting about him, something about him that smelled like danger to the deepest part of her brain.

She didn't call him when she moved to the city. But then the restaurant where she worked as a server was set to shut down, and she discovered that her roommate had been stealing her rent money instead of paying the landlord when a 10-day eviction notice was posted on the door. And so, desperate to avoid the street, she called him.

She'd spent two long years on Kyle's couch, listening to him brag about his Excel spreadsheets and avoiding his increasingly blatant attempts to fuck her. Finally, just as it was becoming unbearable, she'd finally scrimped and saved enough for a deposit for her own apartment. She'd moved as many of her things out of his condo as she could while he was on a two-day all-staff retreat and left without a word, hoping never to see him again.

And yet, here he was, lying to everyone. And they seemed to believe him.

After all, he was a tall, handsome man in a good suit. Who wouldn't?

I knew it was too good to be true.

She looked over at Nellie, who was looking at the receptionist now: still motionless and expressionless, except for a strange eye-twitch that must have been from shock.

Alessandra was sick with wordless despair. Everything she had been working for, the company, the contract, the gateway to her wildest fantasies, her burgeoning love for her beauty and her beast... it was all falling apart.

"I *said*, Allie," snarled Kyle, "let's go home."

Devastated, Alessandra hung her head low and began to follow Kyle away from her new life and back into the grime and misery of her old.

12

Kyle reached out with one clammy hand to grip Alessandra's arm as he steered her towards the elevators. He clamped down with strong fingers, pinching Alessandra's flesh hard. Alessandra let out a small whimper.

Suddenly, there was a great roar from the mouth of a hallway nearby, as if a hawk's call was amplified a thousand times and run through Metallica's sound board.

"What the *fuck?*" shouted Kyle.

An enormous dark shape barrelled out of the depths of the hallway. With a mighty leap and a vicious snarl, Tristan Black launched his two-ton gorgosaur body at Kyle's tall slim one.

Kyle tried to evade the crush of the prehistoric megafauna, but it was far too late; humans cannot outrun wild animals, as a rule, and this was no exception. The man squealed like a tire in an underground parking lot as Tristan's rear talons eviscerated him and pinned him to the ground beneath him.

The squeal turned to a hoarse cry of pain. "Help!" screamed Kyle. "Help! Allie, help me! What the fuck! What the fuck! What the *fuck* is this thing?! This fucking hurts so much, oh my God, what the fuck!" He broke down into racking sobs, blood spurting from torn arteries with every beat of his fading heart.

Alessandra's mouth was open in shock. She was agog at what was happening before her. Was Tristan... protecting her? Even though Kyle had come in and claimed to be her boyfriend?

Was it possible that Tristan actually believed her? Was it possible that, finally, she had someone in her life who was loyal to her? Who prioritized her over the invisible God they prayed to, or over the vagaries of their cock? Could it really be that Tristan *had her back*?

Alessandra looked at the collapsed form of the almost-former Kyle as he bled out on the ground. She couldn't help but feel a little sorry for him. It was a terrible way to go, and she was human, after all. An omnivore, not a carnivore. She had some empathy.

But he had tried to ruin her life. So... fuck him.

Alessandra crouched down next to Kyle's head as Tristan Black squished the life from his body. She wrinkled her nose. Ripped-open intestines smelled *foul*.

"This is Tristan Black," Alessandra said with a smile. "The billionaire philanthropist. *He* is my boyfriend. He's also a gorgosaur, like the dinosaur. A real one. And he's a carnivore."

Blood bubbled up between Kyle's lips as the light faded from his eyes.

"At least your body won't go to waste," Alessandra whispered into the last moments of his consciousness. "And you know, technically, you'll end up being part of Tristan's body if he eats you. You are what you eat, right? So I guess, in a roundabout way, pretty soon you'll get to fuck me after all."

Alessandra's laughter followed Kyle into the dark. It was the last thing he ever heard.

13

"I really thought you didn't believe me," said Alessandra to Nellie, champagne flute in hand.

The two women had snuck into a dark corner at a Black Incorporated charity gala, one of the many hosted by the company each year. This one was a benefit for the local zoo, where one of the female Siberian tigers had just given birth to three perfect cubs. Tristan Black had always wanted to eat a tiger, but he was far too civilized to eat endangered animals, so he preferred to fund breeding programs to hopefully bring their population levels back up to where he would one day be able to have a stripey little snack. A dinosaur could dream, after all.

"Of course I believed you," said Nellie in a low tone. "That guy was a creep."

"I know that *now*," said Alessandra. "I just... how did you decide on an eye-twitch as a secret signal?"

"It's subtle," said Nellie, "and easily mistaken for a stress reaction. All of the receptionists are trained on it. There are a few others, too. I'll teach them all to you in due time. We just can't risk the safety of our most precious employees."

"Like you," said Alessandra with a smile. "You're precious to me."

Nellie leaned in and kissed Alessandra sweetly, slipping in a bit of tongue at the end for some heat. "And you're precious to me. And Tristan. We'd never let you be carted off by some asshole named Kyle." She checked her Apple Watch. "Actually? Let's get out of here. Tristan wants to see you."

Alessandra's heart and clit beat together in anticipation as she let Nellie lead her to the elevator and press the button. They emerged into a space Alessandra had never seen: a massive marble hall lit by an enormous crystal chandelier. It must have been on the very top floor.

And it was nearly filled with roses. There must have been thousands of them.

Tristan Black stood at the centre of the hall. For the first time, he seemed almost small, dwarfed by the scale of the space around him. But to her, he filled the world.

She was speechless. Tears welled in her eyes at the beauty of the scene: the marble, the roses, the beautiful woman beside her. And her lover, her protector, her billionaire, her dinosaur.

"Your performance at work has been exceptional," murmured Nellie beside her, as she led Alessandra toward Tristan. "As has your performance outside of work. And Tristan, it seems, has a more… robust offer for you. One that I think you are likely to accept."

On cue, Tristan reached one of his taloned hands towards Alessandra. In his palm was a small velvet box. He *mrrr*ed to Nellie, who took the box from him and opened it towards Alessandra.

Inside was the most beautiful ring she'd ever seen in her life: an enormous princess-cut diamond solitaire in a simple platinum setting. The diamond was pure white and absolutely flawless. It sparkled with the light of a million stars, of a hundred million years of history.

"This diamond was found near the place where Tristan's ancestors lived," murmured Nellie. "Very likely, the carbon is from some of their bodies, compressed over time into the gem you see here. I suppose you might call it a family heirloom."

Tears welled in Alessandra's eyes. Speechless, she looked at Tristan, and then Nellie.

"And, of course, we're a package deal, Tristan and I. We both adore you, Alessandra. Will you marry us?"

The tears began to fall freely. Before Nellie could say anything else, Alessandra grabbed Nellie's hand and rushed them both into Tristan's small but mighty gorgosaur arms.

"Yes, yes, yes, yes," sobbed Alessandra. "A million times, yes. Of course I'll marry you both. Of course I'll be with you. You are the loves of my life. My heart, my body, my soul are yours."

And with that, the three of them fell into each other with a mighty cry and roar, a passionate kiss of lip and tongue and tooth, a crush of the most powerful force on earth, the most powerful force in all of history: true love.

EXCLUSIVE EXCERPT

DINO STUD

Up close, the Tyrannosaur's breath was even worse than Tallulah had imagined it could be: a charnel-house blast of decaying meat.

Instinctively she recoiled, scrambling back on hands and knees into the shelter of the shipping container, trying to hide from the monstrous reptile as it pushed its muzzle in through the door. As of yet, it seemed not hungry so much as curious about this tiny female intruder into its domain.

Huddled against the rear metal wall, heart hammering, Tallulah stared out at the glittering eye of the giant saurian as it peered in at her. Maybe if she stayed completely still, it would just go away. If she could only control her terrified trembling...

The creature opened its jaws and bellowed. Inside the container the sound was deafening, obliterating. Tallulah covered her ears and screamed.

Was this how it was going to end? Devoured by a dinosaur? Her mind flashed to the chain of events that had led her to this lethal impasse. She really had put herself in this situation for a man.

But not just any man. Reid.

And worse: given the chance to do it over, she knew she'd do the same thing.

Her fugue was interrupted by a vertiginous heave as the dinosaur worked its tail underneath the container, tilting it forward.

And then sudden vertigo, as the enraged beast picked up the container with its powerful arms, tilting it further.

Tallulah felt herself begin to slide towards the opening, towards the waiting jaws that would crush her, the sharp yellow teeth that would tear her to pieces.

She didn't even have the breath to let out another shriek...

Chapter 1

Tallulah finally found the Ranch on her fifth day in Independence, Missouri, after four days of odd glances and raised eyebrows when she asked where it was.

The waitress at Denny's had giggled as soon as she'd heard the name. "Oh, *that* place. Not sure you really want to go there. Those folks are…" She trailed off as she plunked a plate of eggs and whole-wheat toast down in front of Tallulah. "I'm sure they're lovely people. Just keep to themselves. Coffee?"

"Sure," said Tallulah. "What do you mean, they keep to themselves?"

"We just don't see 'em much," said the waitress. Her broad grin was friendly, and her eyes were sharp. "Not for years, in fact. Are you planning to stay long? I think my landlord's got a vacancy coming up at the beginning of the month. Nice little apartment. It's in town."

"Thanks. I'm just here for the summer, but I'll keep it in mind."

"You do that, darlin'. I'll keep an eye out for you."

The next day, at the post office, the clerk had a similar reaction when she asked about the Dino Ranch while buying stamps. "I don't know much about those folks," he'd said, as she was rifling through her handbag to find her wallet. "They don't come into town. Not for a very long time."

"How do they get supplies, do you think?"

The clerk snorted. "Oh, they're *dino* people. They probably have their own special mail-order stores. I don't think they need to follow the same rules as the rest of us."

"Maybe they just get Amazon deliveries."

"Maybe." The clerk fixed Tallulah's eyes with his. He was an older man, sixtyish, with thinning hair and a round face; like the waitress, his eyes were sharp and watchful. "Either way, I don't know that a girl like you needs to get mixed up with folks like that."

Tallulah thanked him, stuffed the stamps in her bag, and headed out into the sunshine.

It was a late-May afternoon. Schoolchildren ran down the sidewalk with their backpacks hanging from one shoulder, shouting and clamoring for after-school treats from their weary-looking parents. Sunlight glinted dustily off the hoods of ten-year-old Chevys and Chryslers. A few cyclists in spandex and bike helmets, obvious work-from-home urban transplants, rested at an intersection and reached into their panniers for snacks.

All the hustle and bustle of a reasonably prosperous small town in farm country.

There was no sign that this was the closest town to the most innovative, and the most dangerous, dino-breeding facility this side of the Mississippi.

Tallulah had read about the Ranch in a travel guide to the area that she'd found deep in the Buzzfeed archives. "The 18 Weirdest Places in Missouri": the Ranch was number seventeen.

"By now we're all so used to the Jurassic Park-ification of our daily lives that a dinosaur ranch seems almost commonplace," the article said. "But this one is different. It's called 'the Ranch'; like Madonna or Lizzo, it needs only one name. The dinosaurs' keepers insist on a 'barn-free lifestyle on hundreds of acres.' It's the closest you'll ever be to the true American West, but instead of buffalo and cowboys, you'll see a greater variety of dinosaurs than any other independent ranch in the state – and the only *T. rex* hatchery in the entire country, other than Dinosys in NYC and Beecee in Arizona."

When she showed it to her parents, they were naturally concerned. "That just doesn't seem safe," her father had said. "A *T. rex* hatchery? Have you ever seen one of those things in person?"

"Obviously not," said Tallulah. "No one has. Almost. But I'm a *paleontology student*, Dad."

"Yes, and when you first chose that path, there was no such thing as a living *T. rex*."

"That's why it's so cool!" cried Talluah. "I went to school to study dinosaurs, and when I started, all you could study was bones. And now, five years later, I can study real live dinosaurs. Who gets to do that?! Whose academic field ever changes that much?"

"I'll tell you what," called Tallulah's mother from the kitchen, "at least we know Lulu won't ever be unemployed."

"Small favors," grumbled her father. "Doesn't do much good to be employed if you're going to be eaten by a *T. rex* ."

"I'm not going to be eaten by a *T. rex* ," sighed Tallulah. "They've got safety protocols at these places."

"Have you even talked to these Ranch people?" asked her father.

"Not yet," Tallulah admitted. "They don't have a website or a phone number or anything. I'm just going to find out where it is and show up."

"So you don't have a job there yet. There's still time to cancel your trip."

"Wasn't it you who always told me to just show up, because that's more than 95% of people ever do?" Tallulah asked, more calmly than she felt.

"You did say that," Tallulah's mother called from the kitchen.

"I am twenty-five years old. I am a PhD candidate at the University of Missouri. I am a grown woman and I am going to show up at "the Ranch" and demonstrate to them that I can be a valuable asset for the summer. I don't need email. I'm going to do this the old-fashioned way."

Tallulah's father leaned back in his recliner and studied his daughter, standing before him in the sun-filled living room of the St. Louis house they'd lived in since before she was born.

He'd always been impressed at how much determination fit into her pint-sized body, ever since she was a child; she'd always been full to bursting with willfulness. It had been a mighty project to help her direct that powerful will into a drive to succeed. And now, he realized ruefully, he was seeing the end result: a young woman who knew what she wanted and would not give up until she had it.

"Alright, then," he said. "You've got my blessing."

"Thanks, Dad," Tallulah said with a smile. "That means a lot. But you know I would have done it either way."

"I know, Chicken," he said, rising from his recliner. He wrapped her in a bear hug just like he had when she was a child, using her childhood nickname. "That's why I love ya."

Now, in the bedroom of the Airbnb apartment she'd rented for two weeks, she was writing a postcard to her parents.

Did you know that chickens and other birds are descended from dinosaurs? They're theropods, like T. rex. Just smaller. And did you know that Independence is where Mormons believe the Garden of Eden was? There are so many little signs that this is the right path for me. Or, if not THE right path, at least it's some kind of right path. I'm going to learn so much this summer at the Ranch. I'll have conference presentations for years! Love you both.

Thought I'd send this the old-fashioned way, because there's nothing like getting real mail.

Your Tallulah.

She drew a tiny stick-figure chicken next to her name, affixed a stamp, and headed back out to the post office to drop it in the mailbox. It was only a fifteen-minute walk through Independence's old downtown. There were a few boarded-up storefronts along with little local businesses, and a few number of chain stores: Dollar Tree, Walgreens, the standard fast-food joints. But despite these encroachments of modernity, and despite

Independence's proximity to Kansas City right next door, she felt its small-town-ness like a bright spot, like a beacon. There was something here for her, she was sure of it.

Something close by, anyhow.

"Hey!" shouted someone from behind her, just as she reached the post office.

Tallulah spun, long brown hair whirling around her face. A tall, freckled teenage boy in basketball shorts and a baggy T-shirt was jogging towards her. "I think you dropped this," he said breathlessly, holding out the postcard.

"Oh, my gosh," Tallulah groaned. "How did I manage that? Thanks so much."

The boy stopped and glanced down at the postcard. "You're welcome, uh, Tallulah. Wait a second. You're going to the Ranch?"

Tallulah held out her hand. "It's not polite to read other people's mail."

"In my defense, this is a postcard," said the boy with a half-smile.

"Fair enough. Give it."

The boy handed it over. "Are you really going to the Ranch? I don't think people are supposed to go there anymore."

"Why?" Tallulah asked.

He shifted uncomfortably. "I don't rightly know, exactly. We just aren't supposed to go there. I think something happened with the lab."

"Where's 'there'? Can you at least tell me where the Ranch is?"

"Out Norborne way, if I recall," said the boy. "My brother went there for a field trip once. But that was years ago. No one really talks about the Ranch anymore."

"Norborne," said Tallulah. "Thank you so much... what's your name?"

"I'm Connor," said the boy. "Hey, can I ask you a favor?"

"What's that?"

"Please don't talk to anyone else about the Ranch, ok? It's just one of those things. People get nervous. It's not good."

Tallulah nodded, suddenly self-conscious. "Got it. Thanks, buddy."

As Connor ran off ahead, Tallulah's mind was racing with anxiety… and excitement. All the local secrecy around the Ranch only made it more enthralling for her. What mysteries could possibly be hiding out there?

What paleontological wonders would she discover, once she found it?

It could make her career. It could make her *life*.

She dropped the postcard into the mailbox and headed straight back to her Airbnb. *Norborne way*, she thought. *See you tomorrow, Ranch.*

Chapter 2

I'm really glad I filled up on wiper fluid, thought Tallulah, less than an hour into her journey. The windshield of her little blue Kia seemed perpetually covered with a fine brown dust that blew across the highway from the fields on either side, despite rows and rows of sprouting green crops. The sun shone down hard and bright. Tallulah donned her darkest pair of sunglasses and put on the "Summer Sunshine" playlist she'd been carefully building for this trip.

There was no way she'd let anyone, or anything, get her down. She was on her way to the Ranch.

She hadn't quite known how to dress for this... ambush. Field khakis? A professional pencil skirt and blouse? She'd ended up settling on something in between: wide-leg khaki pants with a crisp button-down shirt tucked in, her brown hair pulled back into a sleek ponytail that hung halfway down her back, and just enough makeup to look awake and eager: a swipe of black mascara to frame her green eyes, a bit of gloss to enliven her lips. She knew she often looked younger than her age, being as short as she was, but her fieldwork had filled her out and given her a solid, strong build. No one would ever call her *slight* anymore, and she loved it. She wanted to look like the kind of woman who would be able to do anything asked of her.

A woman who was suitable for physical pursuits.

And then, so rickety and faded that she almost missed it, there was the sign for Norborne, Missouri. It seemed almost an afterthought along the highway, with its peeling paint and weathered wood, as if the town couldn't quite believe that anyone would want to know where it was.

The night before she'd set off, at her Airbnb, Tallulah had spent some time with the Google Maps aerial view. She'd searched every building, every landmark, every field within ten miles of Norborne to find any evidence of Dino Ranch, since it wasn't marked on the map. She knew that farm country was characterized by wide open spaces – as the Dixie Chicks merrily sang on her "Summer Sunshine" playlist – but she'd grown up in St. Louis, and her city-girl heart was still astounded at the sheer number of falling-down barns and fallow fields.

And then she spotted it: a hulking shape in a copse of trees by the edge of a pond. She switched to street view to confirm her sighting, hoping against hope that the car-mounted camera had been powerful enough to capture what she thought it was, that the angle was right.

It was. The thing was barely visible, and it seemed to be hiding in the shadow of a big willow tree whose branches drooped down to kiss the water. It was a remarkably beautiful scene, actually. The trees, the little puffs of cloud reflected in the pond, the reeds and grass that bent in the wind along the banks.

And the T-Rex, gazing out across the modern landscape with its glittering prehistoric eye.

She had figured out from there which buildings must be the Ranch, and now she turned from the dusty country road down an even dustier unmarked driveway. It led down a small incline and then up and over a hill. The picturesque pond and willow tree from Google Maps was just about half a mile down the road on the same side; she could see it, faintly, from here.

Tallulah knew from her scrutiny of the map that the Ranch was beyond the hill, and yet her heart beat hard and fast as she thought about cresting that ridge. What if she was wrong? Or worse: what if she was right, and the Ranch had set up a security perimeter of dinosaurs that could crush her Kia flat?

She glanced at her driver's side mirror. OBJECTS IN MIRROR ARE CLOSER THAN THEY APPEAR. "I guess I'll see you if you're comin'," she said out loud with a laugh, and began to drive.

Everything was silent. Even the dusty wind seemed oddly still as she slowly drove down into the dip, then up towards the top of the hill.

At the crest, she had to take a moment to stare.

The hill was not just a hill, but rather the edge of a huge bowl, probably a mile or more across, that was full of strange vegetation. Bushes the size of trees. Plants with enormous fan-shaped leaves, bigger than six of her laid end-to-end. Tall grasses gone to seed, higher than her head, and massive, primitive-looking reeds that ringed a circular pond - more like a lake - in the center. It was incredibly beautiful, and also faintly disturbing in its uncanniness, as if she was looking directly into the distant past of this patch of land, millions of years ago.

And then there was an alarm.

It started as a flash of impossibly bright light, which was followed by a loud, animal shriek. Faintly, she could hear a bell ringing from a building that she hadn't noticed, low and squat and hidden among the leaves and reeds.

Tallulah braced herself. For what, she wasn't quite sure, but it didn't sound good. *Wits about you, Chicken,* she thought. *Let's just ride this out and see.*

Three black cars sped towards her on a track that emerged from the jungled bowl. They stopped a dozen feet from the Kia, and a tall, muscled man emerged from one. His face was a dark cloud, and his body was taut and ready for a fight.

He was the most beautiful man Tallulah had ever seen.

There was another flash of bright light, and then everything was dark.

Chapter 3

Tallulah awoke slowly to the sound of voices in another room. She couldn't quite make out what they were saying, but one sounded contrite. The other, booming and deep, was angry. Not explosively so; he was clearly keeping his anger in check. But he was not happy.

Eyes still closed, she wiggled her fingers and toes. Everything seemed to be in working order. She shifted her body and found herself at the edge of a comfortable mattress, head cradled by a soft pillow. She opened her eyes slowly, as the light in the room was bright - sunshine, she saw, as it streamed in from a large window set into the wall across from the bed.

A large, *barred* window.

Tallulah swung her legs over the edge of the bed, pausing briefly to let the spinning sensation pass, and tentatively stood up. Her body seemed undamaged, to her relief. The room was small, with four cot-style beds and two desks, nothing on the walls except a standard schoolroom-style clock, and a heavy-looking door.

She grabbed the doorknob and tried to turn it. Locked.

As she rattled the doorknob, the voices in the other room immediately stopped. "Hello?" she called out.

After all, if they were going to kill her, they'd probably have done so already. She'd learned that from all the action films she'd watched with her dad over the years, him in his favorite recliner and her on the couch, passing a bowl of popcorn between them.

If she was alive and unharmed, she was valuable to them in some way.

You bet your ass I'm valuable, she thought. *I'm gonna be a paleontologist and I'm at the top of my class.*

There was movement from the other room, and then a key in the lock. "Get away from the door," the deep voice said. "I don't want you coming out here without my permission."

"Yes, sir," said Tallulah sweetly.

After a moment, the door swung open. In the doorway stood the man from the car.

He was tall - at least six foot three - and muscled like a fighter. His shoulders were broad and strong in his casual T-shirt, and his powerful legs threatened to rip his field khakis apart. He had a slight belly, in the manner of men whose strength is practical rather than for show, but it only made him more intriguing to her.

This was not a vain man. This was a man who *got shit done.*

His hair was chin-length and straight, with slightly ragged edges, as if he'd tried to cut it himself and failed so hadn't bothered anymore. It was sandy-blond and sun-streaked like a surfer's. His eyes were a deep blue-grey in a suntanned face that was surprisingly open. His beauty was not cruel or hard, but rather inviting, alluring.

As if he were hungry for the world, and wanted nothing more than to feast on it.

Tallulah had never seen anything so beautiful in her life.

Tallulah and the man sat across from each other at a small table in what passed for a living room at the Ranch. He'd asked the contrite-voiced person, who was small and short-haired and generally amiable, to fetch some coffee for the two of them; rather than ask for milk or sugar,

Tallulah drank hers black, looking directly into those blue-grey eyes as she took her first sip.

"Now that you've got me here, can I at least have your name?" she said to the man.

"I don't think you're in any position to be asking much of anything," he said.

"Oh?" Tallulah said. "Last I checked, false imprisonment was a crime."

"So's trespassing." The man took a sip of coffee, and then another, deeper one.

"Touché".

"I'll make you a deal," said the man, his voice rumbling. Tallulah breathed deeply.

"What's that?"

"You can go on your way, no harm no foul, as long as you swear never to come back here. And never to talk about the Ranch."

"I don't think I like that deal," said Tallulah.

"Oh?"

"I came here for a reason, you know."

"And what's that?"

"I want a summer job."

There was immediate shocked laughter from the the kitchen, and an amused smile from the man. "Don't make the girl feel bad," the man called into the kitchen, and then turned back to Tallulah. "Sorry. They're a bit out of practice when it comes to interaction with outsiders."

"Who is that?"

"They're my assistant. Don't worry. They don't mean to be rude."

"They – so they/them, right?"

"That's right," said Reid.

"And what about you?"

He laughed, a deep rumble. "He/him. I'm just a man."

You certainly are, Tallulah thought. His presence was like a gravity well, drawing her in.

"I need to be clear, though, about something else," said the man. "Did you say you wanted a *summer job*?"

"I did."

"Do you know where you are?"

"If my Google Maps skills are any indication," said Tallulah, "this is the Ranch."

"You are correct," said the man. "But do you know what the Ranch is?"

"You raise dinosaurs in a barn-free lifestyle. You've got the biggest variety of dinos in this part of the country. You've got the only T-Rex hatchery outside of New York and California. And," Tallulah said, "I know it's true, because I saw your *T. rex* on Google Maps."

The man stared at her.

"Street view," Tallulah said. "He was hiding in some trees. The *T. rex.*"

The man picked up his coffee cup, considered taking a sip, and put it down again. He sighed heavily, tangling his fingers in his hair, forehead in his palm. "You're no slouch."

"Nope." Tallulah fought the urge to bask in the compliment. *Be professional.*

"Tallulah Cole," he said.

"Wait. How do you know *my* name?"

"It's on your driver's license. I had a look."

"Right."

"Tallulah. You know what scarecrows are, right?"

"I'm from Missouri," she said. "Also, I've seen *The Wizard of Oz.*"

"Think of that T-Rex like a scarecrow. It's a real *T. rex*, all right, but it's not there for its own sake."

"What do you mean?"

The afternoon sun streamed in past gauzy curtains and metal bars, illuminating the room: a few mismatched couches, a coffee table bearing a plastic-looking fern, the small wooden dining table across which they faced each other, a sturdy-looking door to the outside. Nondescript and strangely comfortable.

"I mean," the man said, "that the T-Rex was there to scare off things that are even bigger. *Much* bigger. And even more… carnivorous."

There was silence for a moment as Tallulah pretended that she wasn't panicking on the inside. Gorgeous man aside, what in the world had she gotten herself into?

What in the world - in all of world history - was bigger and more carnivorous than *Tyrannosaurus Rex*?

A small smile teased the corners of the man's mouth. His skin was sun-kissed and his beard-stubble framed a strong jaw and full, wide lips. Tallulah tried hard not to stare. "You sure you still want a summer job at the Ranch?"

Tallulah took a deep breath and fixed her face into a jaunty grin. "That depends. Is there hazard pay?"

The man laughed, and suddenly the tension in the room seemed to melt away, though Tallulah's magnetic attraction to the man rushed in to take its place. He was *so* gorgeous. "I think we can arrange that."

"In that case, yes. I do. Is this my interview?"

"Oh, you've passed your interview," the man said in his deep voice. "It's been a while since we've had someone new on the team. But I think you'll fit in well here. Fearless to a fault. It's not a common trait."

"I'm not a common girl." Tallulah shocked herself with her own boldness.

"That much is apparent," said the man. "Maybe you'll even make it through the whole summer here."

"There's just one thing I need before I accept your offer," Tallulah said, slyly.

"What's that?"

"I can't take a job with someone whose name I don't know."

"Ah, yes," said the man. He held out his hand to shake hers. "Reid Canmore, your new boss. Pleased to make your acquaintance, Tallulah Cole."

To Be Continued in

DINO STUD

Lola Faust

Also by Lola Faust:

Wet Hot Allosaurus Summer

Triceratops and Bottoms

Tyrannosaurus Sext

How Stego Got His Groove Back

All I Want for Christmas is Utahraptor

Don Juan Velociraptor

Dino Stud

ABOUT THE AUTHOR

"A whole world of romance: erotic novels where humans and dinosaurs are f******, and it's so rad."

-Devendra Banhart

From an early age Lola Faust's fantasies and reveries tilted towards the baroque, the unusual, and the eccentric. Though she entertained curious private journals, it wasn't until she entered the Paleontology program at the University of British Columbia that her fantastic and romantic notions concerning dinosaurs took full flight. While working towards her doctorate, Ms Faust began writing her signature saurian prose. Today she is employed by day at a leading university in her field, but maintains her anonymous and risque personality online. She can be reached at lolafaust1984@gmail.com

Made in United States
Troutdale, OR
12/04/2024